The
SECRET
of the
BLUE
GLASS

The SECRET of the BLUE GLASS

Tomiko Inui

TRANSLATED BY GINNY TAPLEY TAKEMORI

PUSHKIN CHILDREN'S BOOKS

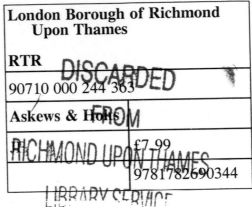

Pushkin Children's Books
71–75 Shelton Street, London, WC2H 9JQ

Text by Tomiko Inui © Shinya Shimizu 1959
Published by Fukuinkan Shoten Publishers, Inc., Tokyo, Japan in 1967 under
the title of *Kokage No Ie No Kobitotachi* (Yuri and the Little People)
The English rights arranged with Fukuinkan Shoten Publishers, Inc. Tokyo.

All rights reserved.

Translation © Ginny Tapley Takemori 2015

First published by Pushkin Children's Books in 2015

0 0 1

ISBN 978-1-782690-34-4

Set in Berling Nova by Tetragon, London

Proudly printed and bound in Great Britain by TJ International, Padstow,
Cornwall, on Munken Pure 120gsm

www.pushkinpress.com

Contents

PRELUDE

———

Everyone has their own special place, a place somewhere on Earth that is theirs and theirs alone—a magical place wherein dwell those important to them, those they love the most.

One such special place was a small valley amidst the sand dunes of the Sahara Desert, a magical setting out of bounds to anyone other than the person who created it, a little prince from an asteroid, a rose and a fox.

Another special place was the delightful riverbank shimmering with the silvery undersides of willow leaves where, far from the dusty world of humans, a small water rat had made his spotless home and a faddish toad had his grand hall—and where, one summer's night just before dawn, the water rat and his friend the mole heard the clear strains of a piper, and found themselves drawn along the river by the beauty of the music ultimately to encounter the luminous figure of Pan in the hush of daybreak.

My special place is a house built in the shade of a large zelkova tree, and home to a big boy, a younger boy and a very small girl of about five or six. The garden is a riot of fruit trees, apricots and chestnuts and figs and cherries.

On clear summer days when the afternoon sun floods the lawn with light, the children take out the hosepipe sprinkler to spray the lawn, and frolic about noisily under the shower of water. The boys are wearing black shorts and the girl a yellow swimsuit her mother made for her. Small rainbows dance over the green turf as the water sprays all around.

My younger self slips out of the house next door and sneaks into the garden. The older middle-school boy and the little girl wave to me in welcome, but the more reserved younger boy scowls. I suck in my breath, and charge into the spray of water.

Oh, the wonder of a cold shower under the dazzling sun on a hot day! Intoxicated by summer, we roll around the lawn like young braves. The fragrance of wet grass, the sweet smell of damp earth... Finally the smaller boy pounces on me like a young bear and we start wrestling with all our might. The little girl's eyes glitter merrily as an imp's as she watches us, her happy laugh ringing high up in the branches of the big tree.

After a while the sky darkens and a real afternoon shower comes along, putting an end to our play. A loud clap of thunder rumbles through the sky, and the little girl and her two elder brothers vanish into the darkness. And so does my younger self.

It is always midsummer in my special place.

At times, little scamp that I am, I am up in the white fig tree in the girl's garden. Playing the part of a robber, I clamber over our cypress hedge, climb the tree and move from one fruit to the next, milky-white sap seeping from the stalks as I pick them, devouring them greedily as I go. The air is filled with the fragrance of the fig leaves.

The little girl comes out of her quaint Western-style house. *Oh no!* I hide my face under the big leaves, but she makes a beeline for the tree and politely calls up, "Pick one for me too!" The fearless robber is instantly transformed into an angel descended from heaven to pick a fig. "Thank you!" she says gratefully and, skipping over the short shadows, goes back into the house.

My mind full of the girl with a slim neck and beads of sweat on her nose, I sit on my fig branch drawing a castle in the blue sky, a daydream castle where one day the girl and I will live together. As the big summer thunderclouds amass and begin to tower high, so too my castle spreads throughout the boundless blue sky.

In my own special place there is no little prince from a distant star, nor a pleasant riverbank from where sound the clear strains of Pan's pipes. My special place is the house in Tokyo where I was born and grew up, which was destroyed in an air raid during the war. I can still recall how, when I joined the mass evacuation of primary school children leaving for the countryside, I kept looking back at it longingly over my shoulder as I was led away. No trace remains of that house now, nor of the house in the shade of the big zelkova tree next door. And I'll probably never again get to meet that little imp of a girl who lived there.

Or so I believed for over ten years, until one day I ran into an old friend by chance on the train and he happened to mention her to me. "She still remembers you, you know. She said she sometimes wishes she could meet up with that boy next door who was so good at the high bar. She sounded really quite wistful."

I was speechless. Paying me no heed, my friend went on, "It really took me back, talking about our childhood days with her. Although she didn't say much, really. She'd probably have talked more if you'd been there. She always did seem to like you better than me." As a boy he had always been kind, if a bit tactless, and he hadn't changed in that respect. "Why don't you pay her a visit? This is where she said she's staying." He wrote an address on a scrap of paper and passed it to me.

He seemed to want to carry on reminiscing and if I'm honest, I did want to hear more about what the girl was doing now. However, I just couldn't bear the thought of someone else barging in on my special place, and so I took my leave of him.

As I made my way home, I ripped up the scrap of paper he'd given to me into little pieces. I wanted to remain for ever the lively, wild boy doing endless spins up on the high bar the way she remembered me! And I wanted her always to be the little imp of a girl in my special place.

The tiny shreds of paper scattered in the breeze.

A few months later, I came across a small package in the mail at work one morning. As I turned it over to see the name of the sender, thinking it must be a submission from a reader, my hands started shaking. Written there in blue Magic Marker was: "Yuri Moriyama", the name of the little girl in my special place.

I tore into the package, opened the large notebook and started reading. That little girl next door had had an altogether more magical place of her own! I felt I was being shown another, hitherto hidden, dimension to my own special place as I was drawn into her story.

THE LITTLE BOOK ROOM

There was once a small library on the first floor of a house. It was at the end of a long, dark corridor, in the most inconspicuous, quietest corner of all the house. Its heavy oak door was rarely opened, and for the most part remained firmly closed as if to discourage anyone from entering.

Whoever did push open the door would find a little room with three walls entirely covered from floor to ceiling with bookshelves stuffed full with all manner of books that lorded it over the room with a self-important air. Crammed in beside antiquated tomes written in classical Chinese were the Meiji-period works in foreign languages that the grandfather of the house had been so fond of, and next to them were around 200 small paperbacks covered with a light coating of dust.

In short, this was a place where old books, having completed the term of their employment, could peacefully sleep away their retirement.

And it was in this little book room, high up in the triangular space between the sloping ceiling and the top shelf of the bookcase to the right, beside the dormer window, that the Little People had made their home.

Just outside the window were the thick branches of the great zelkova tree in the garden. In summer their dense greenery served as a curtain against the strong rays of the sun, while in winter the bare treetop made way for the sunshine, converting the Little People's home into a warm sunroom.

Other than the rather solemn atmosphere, with its peculiar smell of a mixture of dust, mildew and top-quality paper, there really couldn't have been a better place for the Little People to dwell. It would have been hard to find anywhere else where they could live so quietly and so completely out of the way of prying eyes.

They had come to this house in a Tokyo suburb not long after it was built around the end of the Meiji period, and had remained here uneventfully ever since.

It had been during the summer holidays of 1913, to be precise, that the two British-born Little People had arrived at the house, shaken about in the basket carried by its present owner, Tatsuo Moriyama. Tatsuo had been in primary school at the time, and attended his year-three classes every day dressed in a splash-pattern kimono with *hakama*.

Little Tatsuo had been handed the basket by his English teacher, Miss MacLachlan, just before she boarded a ship from Yokohama headed for home. Miss MacLachlan was an educationist who had come to Japan from England in the 1890s. She taught English at a girls' school in Yokohama, but instead of taking accommodation in the school dormitory, she lived on her own in the suburbs and taught basic English to the local schoolchildren in her spare time.

Now, after twenty years in Japan, she was returning to her home country. When the Moriyama boy, whom she had known since he was a baby, came to say goodbye to her, she immediately ushered him into her now empty house. The animal-patterned carpet that Tatsuo had delighted in walking on whenever he came to this house was now packed away somewhere. The framed pictures that had adorned the walls were all gone, and the room looked quite dreary.

Miss MacLachlan took an old basket from amongst the luggage piled up in one corner and pressed it firmly into the hand of her smallest pupil. "Please make sure the Little People in this basket always get their milk," she told him. "You should place a glass of milk on the windowsill for them once a day. Can you do that?"

She looked steadily into Tatsuo's eyes as he stared at her in astonishment. Miss MacLachlan had come to Japan in her twenties, and now there were white strands appearing in her flaxen hair. She held the boy's gaze with eyes that were a mysterious deep grey.

"Tatsuo Moriyama, you're a boy who loves little birds and insects, and you can keep a promise. Now, will you promise to do as I ask?" She spoke with an intense earnestness.

"Yes miss, I'll give them milk. I'll give them biscuits too sometimes. My mum's biscuits are really good, they'll like them."

Tatsuo's teacher had been telling him fairy stories ever since he was little, and so he knew just what she meant by Little People. And for the first time Miss MacLachlan smiled faintly, just as she did when she listened to Tatsuo's answers in class.

"No, no, they don't need biscuits. The only food these Little People take is milk, and that's the way it's always been. Every day you should fill this glass with milk and put it on the windowsill for them. You mustn't forget now. The Little People cannot live unless humans do this for them. Do you understand?"

Miss MacLachlan took a small glass goblet out of her pocket. It was a beautiful blue, as if a piece of the sky had melted into the glass, and sparkled in the sunlight streaming in through the window, making the gloomy room suddenly seem bright and cheerful.

Tatsuo felt a very slight buzz coming through the basket handle. He stiffened, and looked up at Miss MacLachlan. The teacher abruptly reached out a hand and snapped open the clasps on the old basket. The lid creaked as she opened it a crack, no more than a couple of inches. As the blue light from the glass goblet filtered in, Tatsuo caught sight of two tiny doll-like faces. A barely audible tinkle, like the top keys on the piano, tickled his ears.

The brief, dreamlike moment ended as Miss MacLachlan closed the lid and told him, "They said that they don't mind being seen by you. They have agreed to go with you. Tatsuo, please don't let anyone else see them, and look after them well."

Before he knew what he was doing, Tatsuo had taken the sparkling sky-blue goblet from his teacher. "Goodbye! And have a safe trip!"

Miss MacLachlan gave Tatsuo a parting peck on the cheek and disappeared back into the house.

I'll get to why Miss MacLachlan left the Little People behind in the care of ten-year-old Tatsuo Moriyama when she returned to her country later in the story, but first I'll describe the Little People and their arrival in the Moriyama household.

There were two Little People in the basket. Balbo Ashe, with his sturdy hands, was a shoemaker by trade. His rather timid wife Fern was a stickler for cleanliness, and it was thanks to her good housekeeping that the book room at the Moriyamas' was always free of cobwebs.

Balbo and Fern were not settled into the little book room right away, however. To begin with, Tatsuo put their basket at the back of his toy cupboard where there would be no fear of them being seen by anyone else. But six house mice were also living in that cupboard and the basket proved to be a convenient teeth sharpener for them. The day passed uneventfully, but poor Balbo and Fern had to listen to the terrifying thunder of the mice gnawing away at it all night long.

When Tatsuo brought the milk the next morning and saw the tooth marks on the basket he was so shocked he could hardly breathe. He immediately peeked inside the basket and saw that Balbo and Fern were safe, but they were in such a state of terror that they looked half dead.

He had to find a safe place for them without a moment's delay, and went around the house in search of one. The ground-floor reception room with the piano smelt far too stuffy, but then he remembered the first-floor library where hardly anybody ever went.

Tatsuo ran straight upstairs and down the dark corridor, and pushed open the heavy oak door. Inside, the room was bathed in honey-coloured sunshine streaming in through the window in the roof. He soon found a very pleasant spot in the little triangular space between the top shelf of the tall bookcase and the sloping ceiling, bathed in shimmering light filtering in through the leaves of the zelkova tree.

He rushed back to his own room, wrapped Balbo in his handkerchief and took him to the little book room. Balbo, too, was much taken by its peaceful atmosphere, so Tatsuo went back to his room, gently lifted the basket out of his toy cupboard and carried Fern upstairs. Fern arrived in the little book room clutching onto the luggage that Miss MacLachlan had placed in the basket, pale and exhausted like a migrant who had just survived a rough ocean voyage.

Tatsuo took some books off the shelf and made some secret steps that nobody but he and the Little People would know about. Even if the maid did happen to come into the room to dust the shelves, as long as she didn't actually climb onto the books she wouldn't be able to reach the Little People's home.

It was a few more days before the Little People's home on the bookcase was ready. The basket was too big to fit on the shelf, so Tatsuo had to build their new house himself. When at last it was finished, all anyone looking up at it from below would see was a shelf full of tightly packed books.

Inside he had made comfortable beds for the couple with two empty Gelbe Sorte cigarette boxes that he had sneaked out of his father's study. He gave some pink and white scraps of soft silk from the drawer of his mother's sewing machine to Fern, who used her own needle to sew them into curtains for their bedsteads. With what was left over, she made some charming undergarments for her baby, soon to be born.

Tatsuo enjoyed spending the summer days devising ways to complete the house for the Little People. Balbo and Fern were still not entirely comfortable with being seen by Tatsuo, and so they busied themselves with their handiwork out of his sight.

Every day Tatsuo would fill the blue glass goblet with milk, climb to the top of the bookcase and place the goblet on the sill of the dormer window where there was no fear of it being noticed from outside. He never tired of seeing how the rather sombre interior of the little book room would suddenly brighten as the blue glass sparkled in the sunlight.

Thinking about how the lives of these Little People depended on the milk he brought them daily, his heart quickened and he was filled with a proud sense of responsibility. Fern was too high-minded ever to let Tatsuo see how she used the milk in the meals she prepared for the Ashe household, but their baby girl Iris, and then their boy Robin, thrived on the milk he brought them.

Tatsuo continued the milk deliveries for 1,477 days straight, but when he started middle school he handed the role over to his little sister, Yukari. Yukari had already found out some years earlier about her big brother secretly filling the blue goblet with milk and taking it upstairs to the book room, but being a self-effacing child she never asked him about it. Now, however, she saw how late he came home from school every day and realized that delivering the milk had become something of a burden to him, and so she offered to help.

Yukari was a sickly child and often off school, so for some time she had been going to the little book room when Tatsuo wasn't there to read books and magazines. When she started delivering the milk in his place, therefore, the Little People were not afraid of her. Indeed Balbo and Fern thought she was very well behaved and had grown quite fond of her. This new role was a welcome change for Yukari, too. Instead of always being looked after by others, for once she was able to do something for someone else.

Every time she delivered the blue glass goblet and saw how the little book room brightened in its presence, she felt an indescribable happiness well up within her. She started taking clothes and furniture from her own doll's house to the Little People. House-proud Fern gazed around her home, suddenly filled with the shelves, floor lamp and sparkling-clean gas stove, and gave a contented sigh. But Yukari wasn't able to continue caring for the Little People for very long, for the following winter she contracted pneumonia and passed away.

It was around this time that a strange little girl who'd been born abroad came to stay at the Moriyamas'. Tatsuo and Yukari's Uncle Jun, who lived in Australia, sent his twelve-year-old daughter Toko—their cousin—to school in Japan.

Unlike Yukari, Toko was healthy and strong-willed. It took her some time to get used to the rigid style of education in

Japan, and as soon as she got home from school she would steal into the upstairs library and immerse herself in a book. She had always loved reading, and for her the Moriyamas' library was a veritable treasure trove. And, being sharp-eyed, she often caught sight of the Little People.

One day she fixed her steely gaze on Tatsuo and demanded, "Tatsuo, introduce me to those people on top of the bookcase!"

Tatsuo, now fifteen years old, was left blushing and tongue-tied. Since Yukari had passed away, he himself had been delivering the Little People's milk again. He somehow managed to wriggle out of it this time, but that night, after consulting Balbo and the others, he decided to confide his secret to his cousin.

"Promise me you won't tell anyone. And that you'll place the goblet of milk on the windowsill every morning."

"Okay!" Toko looked up at her cousin a little scornfully, but as soon as she took the small blue goblet in her hands she was captivated. After few moments she asked, "When will I get to meet the Little People?"

"If you keep it up for weeks and weeks without ever missing a day, I reckon they'll eventually show themselves to you."

"Okay," said Toko, frowning. "I really like you, Tatsuo. I'll keep my promise for you!"

And so for seventy-seven days in a row, without being seen by either Tatsuo's parents or the maids, Toko left the goblet of milk on the windowsill in the little book room. On the evening of the seventy-seventh day, Iris and Robin came out of the house by the window, and smoothly climbed down onto Toko's shoulder in a gesture of friendliness. Toko was so happy at this show of trust from the two children that she found herself half laughing and half crying.

She continued delivering the milk for a long time thereafter. Iris and Robin were more used to her than anyone else, and when she came there to read books they would always come onto her shoulder. Robin especially liked to swing from her long hair.

She had been delivering the milk for 2,777 days when she married her beloved Tatsuo, by then a university student, and became the young mistress of the Moriyama household.

Twenty years later, in June 1943, Tatsuo Moriyama was an equable forty-year-old scholar of English literature, and his wife Toko a mother of three in her late thirties, and they were of course still living in the house with a little book room shaded by the big zelkova tree in the garden. The house had survived the great earthquake and fire of 1923, although it now looked quite different with an added extension and refurbishments to several rooms and part of the garden. The one corner of the house that had not changed at all was the little book room.

Living peacefully in the house now were Tatsuo and Toko, their son Shin and daughter Yuri, and the family of Little People. Their other son, Tetsu, had that spring just left the house in which he'd lived for seventeen years and was attending a high school in Kyoto.

Even after her marriage to Tatsuo, Toko had continued delivering milk to the Little People. When Tetsu turned eight, after consulting with Balbo and Fern, she handed the role over to her good-natured firstborn. And when Tetsu turned thirteen, he in turn passed it on to his nine-year-old brother Shin.

Unlike Tetsu, who was a considerate boy, Shin was hot-tempered like his mother and rather reserved. He did have his kind side, though, and when he was little he would spend hours watching a damaged ants' nest, and on one occasion rushed out with some raw eggs for the horse of a cart overturned on a slope nearby.

Shin was made to wait a long time before taking over the important role of delivering milk, but when at last he did so, he devised a cover to prevent dust getting into the milk, and adapted the tin-plate toy refrigerator that had belonged to his Aunt Yukari so that it could take a chip of real ice. Thanks to him, that summer Fern could serve up meals made with fresh milk to the Ashe family's dinner table. She was exceedingly grateful that there was no longer any fear of the milk going off.

But there came a time when both Fern and Balbo noticed that Shin's eyes had taken on a cold glint. Fern had been happier than anyone at his solicitude for them, but now she sadly shook her head and said, "What's happened to that boy? I'm starting to feel a bit afraid of him."

Shin had handed the milk delivery over to his little sister Yuri towards the end of the year before, and since turning thirteen he hardly ever showed his face in the little book room. He stayed late at school to study for exams, after which he went to kendo practice where he was apparently the favourite of the PE teacher, a former soldier. Upon starting middle school, he had informed his mother that he would be attending a military preparatory school. Toko had been speechless, and felt a chill creep over her. Not a single Moriyama boy, nor indeed any of the family friends, had ever set their sights on being a soldier. Noting his mother's shock, Shin proudly reassured her that now he had decided his path in life, studying was so much more fun.

On the rare occasions Shin did actually go to the little book room, he would hurriedly pick out some books featuring words like "patriotism" or "military" on the cover and rush out again. Fern and Robin would watch him wistfully from the house by the window, but Shin would pretend he hadn't seen them.

Yuri, who had just turned nine that year, was the Moriyamas' youngest child and a loyal milk-deliverer. Those who had known Aunt Yukari would swear that she had been reborn in Yuri. Even Balbo and Fern, looking at the thin and sickly Yuri, would feel as though the decades had rolled back and it was Yukari there before them.

A long time ago, Yukari had told Balbo and the others, "This room is lovely and quiet, but don't you find it damp and stuffy? Why don't we get Tatsuo to make a hole to let some air in?" But before she could talk to Tatsuo about it, she contracted pneumonia and passed away. Recently, the very same idea had unwittingly occurred to Yuri. If only we could get some fresh air into this dusty book room, how much better life would be for Balbo and his family, she thought. Yuri was stronger than her aunt, and the moment her big brother Tetsu came home from school for the summer holiday, she asked him to make an air hole for them.

Tetsu readily agreed, and immediately fetched some carpentry tools to make a small air hole by the dormer window, along with a little canopy outside to protect it from the rain. Inside he placed a toy fan from Yuri's doll's house. When Balbo and Robin spun the blades as hard as they could, it would keep directing the cooler air into the room for quite some time. For the first time in around thirty years fresh air flowed through the top branches of the zelkova tree and into the little book room. Iris had just started learning how to knit, and now she dyed some spider's silk to make rainbow-coloured ribbons to tie to the fan.

Listening to the excited voices of the Little People, Yuri smiled. "Tetsu, did you use to deliver the milk every day too?" she asked, looking up at her big brother adoringly.

"Me? Of course I did! I started when I was eight and didn't miss a single day in five years... some days I got Mum to help me though. But things haven't changed much in Tokyo yet, have they? There doesn't seem to be any milk shortage here, anyway." Tetsu had grown up in the time he'd been away, and now he gazed down at his little sister sympathetically. "Yuri, I think things are going to get tough from now on. It might be a bit difficult to keep up the milk deliveries."

THE TWO MEN

———

Robin had just celebrated his eighth birthday. Little People developed at the same speed as human children until the age of five, gaining one year of age for every year passed, but after five they grew more slowly, gaining only one year for every five human years. While the members of the Moriyama household were steadily ageing, therefore, both Balbo and Fern were still in their forties. Iris had been born when Tatsuo was still in primary school, but whereas Tatsuo was now forty she was only nine. Even now, both she and Robin were still enjoying their childhood much as they had thirty years ago.

After Balbo had taught him his ABCs, Robin had started learning Japanese writing from a picture book. It was a cute little volume, what humans call a "miniature book", but still it was bigger than he was. It had been a gift to Aunt Yukari from her parents on her fifth birthday. Neither Shin nor Yuri had ever seen it, because Robin had come across it when he was about five or six, and was so taken by it that he had pestered Balbo to bring it back to their little house for him.

Balbo had thoroughly disapproved of taking such a big item from a lower shelf up to their home on the top of the bookcase, but Robin wouldn't listen, and so Balbo and Fern had risked their lives to get it for him. Now they were glad they had done so, for their young son, who had always hated studying, was hard at work every day learning how to read and write Japanese from this book.

"After... walking... through... brush... land for a... thou... sand... leagues, the ti... ger... came to... a place... with no... trees."

In his sing-song voice, Robin read aloud from his favourite page about the tiger. He'd read it hundreds of times before, and could now recognize the same words anywhere, and write them too.

This morning, as always, Robin had stood the book up in the light beneath the dormer window and was reading about the tiger. The balmy September sunlight sparkled as it filtered through the leaves of the big tree outside, and he felt as though he was in a forest. He really felt sorry for the tiger. All the other animals—the polar bear, the deer, the wolf and the wild boar—each had two pages of the book to themselves, and only the tiger was sitting in just one page looking terribly cramped.

"I know! I'll draw in some trees for the tiger in this blank space here."

Robin ran to the storeroom to fetch a green crayon that

Tatsuo had dropped on the floor long ago and Fern, being the thrifty person she was, had squirrelled away. Robin hoisted it onto his back and returned to the book.

"Robin, what are you doing?" called Fern from the kitchen.

"Just studying!"

Apparently satisfied with his answer, Fern nodded and turned back to her work. She and Iris were washing the spider silk they'd gathered from around the little book room and dying it all the colours of the rainbow.

Robin gave a little shrug and then carefully laid the book down flat on its back. He opened it on the page with the tiger, then mounted the green crayon like a horse and began prancing around the page drawing in the vegetation.

Suddenly, from the downstairs front room came the sound of a door being slammed, followed by some unfamiliar voices, alarmingly loud.

Balbo was seated at his worktable, stitching some red shoes for Iris. Fern and Iris were in the kitchen, and Robin was drawing in his book, but they now all stopped what they were doing and pricked up their ears. They could hear Tatsuo, who was normally so quiet, arguing about something. Then came the sound of a number of humans marching around the house. Two sets of footsteps came up the stairs and along the corridor towards the little book room.

Balbo and Fern quickly grabbed the two children and the Little People all vanished into the darkest corner of the bookcase. Robin tried to ask something, but Balbo put his hand over his mouth to silence him.

The heavy oak door swung open and two men came in, the first people outside the Moriyama family to have set foot in the room for decades. The men looked sharply around at the wall-to-wall bookcases and then, as if moving in for the kill, began pulling out books: red-cloth European editions, splendid leather-bound anthologies, dusty old magazines—all thrown roughly onto the growing pile on the floor.

Fern pressed her apron skirt to her mouth to stop herself from crying out. Someone appeared in the doorway and stood coldly watching the two men. It was Toko, the little girl who had grown up in the house and eventually married Tatsuo Moriyama. Now she was dressed plainly in Western-style clothes, her hair cut in a short bob. Biting her lip, she demanded, "Just what to you intend to do with all these old books? Most of them are for children anyway."

"I see. So this is the sort of reading material you give your children, then," said one of the men with distaste, holding up a black book with a Russian title.

"Ah, Kropotkin... actually that one belonged to my father-in-law."

"Whatever. We'll be taking it to the station with us as evidence, anyway."

The two men scooped up the pile of books from the floor and quickly exited the room. Toko followed them out and pulled the door closed after her. Their footsteps faded down the long corridor and then a door slammed in the distance. A long, long silence fell over the house.

Balbo and Fern looked at each other, their faces pale. This was the first time anything so ominous had happened since they came to live in this house all those decades ago. They felt keenly that something terrible was befalling the Moriyama household, although they had no idea what.

Iris buried her face in her mother's skirt in terror. Fern felt sorry for her daughter, who was so timid she rarely even spoke, and reassured her, "Don't worry, everything will be okay. Let's finish up dying the silk thread. 'The busy bee has no time for sorrow', as they say. Those are the words of a great English poet, you know."

Less fearful than Iris, Robin had been more surprised to learn that there were other humans outside the Moriyama family. Then, noticing his parents' subdued mood, he asked worriedly, "We will get our milk tonight, won't we? I hope Yuri doesn't forget!"

"No, I'm sure she won't forget," Balbo said with a sigh, sitting down at his worktable.

That evening, the Little People heard the quiet patter of Yuri's footsteps as she brought them the blue glass goblet on a little tray as usual. After a moment's hesitation upon seeing the shambles in the little book room, she placed the goblet of milk on the sill of the dormer window as she always did. Even on a day like this, the sparkling blue glass lit up the room.

Her eyelids were puffy as though she had been crying, and she muttered something to herself over and over again as she picked the books up off the floor one by one and put them back on the shelves. "Daddy hasn't done anything wrong. Daddy hasn't done anything wrong."

As Balbo and Fern had feared, a dark shadow had fallen on the peaceful Moriyama household. Yuri still came to the little room twice a day, once to collect the empty goblet, and once to bring it back full of milk, but they could see the sadness in her face. Fern began using a little of the milk every day to make cheese that could be stored.

For a long time the Little People didn't know why Yuri was so sad, but then one day she and Shin came into the little book room arguing.

"Daddy *is* bad! He's a liberalist. I've known that for ages. He only respects things from abroad, and says that Japan is making a mistake by going to war. That makes him a traitor, doesn't it? That's why the police took him away. It's his own fault."

"No, you're lying. Daddy hasn't done anything wrong!"

"So why did the police arrest him then, Yuri? It's because he's done something wrong, of course!"

"No, you're lying! You're stupid! The police are stupid! There's no way Daddy would do anything bad."

Balbo and Fern gazed on mournfully as Yuri shouted angrily at her brother, quite unlike her usual self. Shin scanned the bookcases as if looking for something, and then glanced up at the dormer window with a grimace. Fern felt a chill run down her spine.

"Yuri, are you still doing that every day?" Shin asked.

Sobbing, Yuri gave a slight nod, relieved that he had changed the subject. But then Shin went on, "You shouldn't be doing that now, not in these times of crisis! That milk must be from the black market. There are sick soldiers on the battle-front who don't have enough milk to drink, you know!"

Yuri looked at Shin in surprise. Times of crisis? Black market milk? On the battle-front? She had been hearing things like this at school every day, along with slogans like "Don't ask for anything until we've won!" or "Luxury is the enemy!"—but it had never occurred to her that it might have anything to do with the Little People at home. All the children of the Moriyama household had been brought up to take a small amount of milk to the Little People every day without fail to ensure their survival, and they had always done so unquestioningly.

"But Shin, you used to do it too, didn't you?" Yuri stared vacantly at her brother as if he'd suddenly turned into a different species.

"Everyone else is out fighting for our country, but here at home you just don't get it, do you? None of you do!" spat Shin and stormed out of the room. It was as though a pall had fallen over the little book room, despite the gold and green sunlight streaming merrily down on the blue goblet.

In the Little People's home, Fern drew her eyebrows together in a frown and thought it was just as well she had started making cheese to keep in case of emergencies. *I'm going to have to be extra careful not to waste even a drop of milk from now on. Who knows what might happen?*

Balbo had remained seated at his worktable stitching the red shoes for Iris—the leather was top-quality, taken from the cover of an old notebook—during the exchange between Yuri and Shin. He listened without a word, aware that hard times were to come, worse than any they had known before. While they had been enjoying their peaceful life here in the quiet little book room, a terrible storm had apparently been raging outside.

Balbo knew nothing of the unfortunate sequence of events that had happened after the Great Kanto Earthquake of 1923.

He had no idea that numerous battles had been fought, nor that tens of thousands of people had shed blood in a war of Japan's own making, much less that his own native Britain was now Japan's enemy.

But now even the little book room had been affected, with those two men storming in and hauling Tatsuo Moriyama off to the police station, and Tatsuo's own son calling his father a traitor right before Balbo's eyes, and he was suddenly keenly aware of the severity of the storm outside.

He rested his small head, now flecked with grey, on his worktable. *I don't understand. Whatever happened to Shin? He was such a sweet child. No other child of the Moriyama household has ever changed like that, so why him?* He just couldn't understand why Shin had changed. Irritated at his own sense of powerlessness, he picked up the shoe again and started sewing at a furious pace.

"Balbo, don't wear yourself out!" pleaded Fern. "I wonder what Yuri thinks about it all? If she turns into a patriot like Shin, then whatever will become of us?"

Balbo signalled to her that Iris was listening. Iris was seated next to her mother knitting some rainbow-dyed spider silk into beautiful ribbons. Whenever she wasn't cleaning or in the kitchen helping her mother prepare meals, Iris would spend her time knitting. She used the little ivory knitting needles from a shepherdess doll that Fern had inherited from her own mother Beatrice Belladonna Took back in England. Beatrice had taught Fern how to knit and, according to Little People custom, she in turn had passed on the skill to her own daughter. Fern preferred being up and about cleaning or making cheese, and so now Iris did all the knitting and darning for the Ashe household.

Fern turned her gaze from her daughter to her son. Robin had climbed up to the dormer window and was looking intently outside. Fern was about to remind him to get on with his studies, but she held her tongue. *What good will studying do him in any case? There must be something more important for him to learn about than how to read.*

Had they done the right thing by teaching their children that the only people in the world besides themselves were the Big People in the Moriyama family who brought them milk? She sighed and busied herself using a candle to wax the cotton thread that Balbo was using to stitch the shoes so that it wouldn't snag.

Robin was looking at two pigeons sitting on a branch outside the dormer window. He wasn't thinking about his studies, or about his joy at talking with the tiger in that book he liked so much. What he was thinking was, *I need to know about the world outside. Right now I'm locked away in here. I'm hemmed in, just like that tiger!*

His world, which had consisted of just his own family, the Big People in the Moriyama family whose role it was to bring them food, and his magnificent tiger friend in the picture book, had been utterly shattered when those two big men had burst into the little book room. As the days passed, that incident gradually took on more and more importance in his mind. Yuri had been really downcast ever since, and his own father, too, had grown noticeably taciturn. His mother had become even more finicky, and would put any milk that Robin or Iris left undrunk, however little, into a small pot to boil up again for reuse, and used half of all the milk that Yuri brought them to make cheese.

Supposing I got on that pigeon's back and flew up into the big wide sky, what would I see? I might discover that there are more than just four or five people in the world. There might be dozens, or even hundreds!

Robin gazed longingly at the pigeons outside the window. The pair of them, one white and one grey, had been living on that branch for some time now. Even their feet, tightly gripping the branch, looked about three times as big as Robin himself. But Robin remembered having seen a picture of a person riding a big horse over three times their size.

One day I'm going to go outside and make friends with those pigeons. And I'll get them to let me ride on their backs like horses!

First of all, though, he had to come up with a plan to get out of that room onto the roof and into the outside world. After lunch, Balbo and Fern went to bed for their afternoon nap, and Iris sat in her little rocking chair and carried on knitting as usual. As she worked the needles, the ribbon grew longer and longer, and sparkled in the light.

"Iris, I'm just going to have a look at the air vent in the roof. Somehow it doesn't feel like any fresh air is getting in," Robin told his sister.

Iris looked at him curiously, and then nodded as if in agreement.

Robin's heart began pounding. He climbed smoothly up to the ceiling and tried to move the fan that Tetsu had installed in front of the air vent one summer holiday. He shook it with all his strength but it didn't budge an inch, so he climbed through its blades and tentatively looked out through the air vent. The rain cover obscured his view of the sky, and the air flowing down on him was hot but refreshing. He held up his arms and, using his foot to propel himself from the frame covering the fan, he made a leap for the ledge outside the air vent. Being light, and flapping his legs to gain extra distance, he was soon standing beneath the rain cover.

There, bathed in a deluge of sunrays and endless waves of air, Robin discovered how small he really was. Suppressing the urge to yell "Yoo-hoo!", he gazed up at the big tree. Its branches stretched out higher and wider than he'd ever imagined, casting their shade over the black mountainous ridge of the Moriyama house's roof and the garden encircled by dahlias and hollyhocks.

And beyond that, he could see a grove of green trees and an expanse of red, black and blue roofs! If, say, four or five Little People and four or five Big People were living under each of those, that meant there were an awful lot of people in the world!

What's more, if he really strained his eyes, at the bottom of that hill in the distance there were countless more small, black-tiled roofs. And even farther beyond that was the gleaming sweep of the grey-blue sea.

I had no idea! I never knew the world was so big!

Robin's eyes filled with tears.

Iris knew that her little brother had gone through the air vent in the roof and ventured outside—outside where not even Balbo or Fern had ventured even once these past thirty years!

Two minutes passed, five minutes passed, but Robin didn't come back. Iris began to feel afraid. She had just put her knitting to one side and stood up, thinking she had better wake their parents from their afternoon nap, when two little feet appeared in the hole.

Robin looked terribly serious as he went without a word to the corner of the room and stood there staring at the wall. *That boy has seen the outside world... and one of these days, I too will have to see it for myself!*

Iris gazed up at the hole of the air vent, her eyes filled with both fear and longing. Then she got back on with her knitting as if she hadn't noticed anything amiss.

A FAIRY STORY

———

Gradual changes were happening in the little book room as well as outside.

While Balbo and Fern were taking their afternoon nap, Robin worked at widening the opening of the air vent using a chisel and plane from Balbo's toolbox. He wanted to make it big enough for even broad-shouldered Balbo to be able to get through it easily should this ever become necessary.

Robin also made friends with a gentle, grey pigeon by the name of Yahei, one of the pigeons that came to roost on the branches of the big tree.

Robin had been watching it from beneath the rain canopy for a while, so when he noticed that it seemed intensely irritated by an itch behind its wing, since nobody was around he called out to it.

"Hello. Is something wrong?"

The pigeon fixed a round, red eye on the unfamiliar little boy. Then, as if it couldn't stand it any more, said, "Would you be so kind as to scratch my back for me?"

Robin nervously went up to the big bird and with all his might scratched the point at the root of the wing that seemed to be the source of its irritation.

"Coo coo, ooh that feels better!" said Yahei, evidently enjoying the relief. They both began to feel a little more comfortable with each other.

The next day, Robin was happy when, unbeckoned, Yahei left the group of pigeons and flew alone over to him. He seemed to have taken a liking to little Robin's sociable nature.

They hadn't been friends for ten days yet when Robin told Yahei, "I'd love to be able to sit on your back and fly through the sky, even just a little!"

Yahei readily agreed, so Robin plucked up the courage to scramble up his large friend's red leg and up onto his back. But the moment he touched Yahei's feathers, the pigeon flapped his wings and flew away, and he tumbled off onto the roof and hastily clutched hold of a roof tile.

"Sorry! I'm sorry!" Yahei came back apologizing profusely. But his eyes were laughing. "It was just so ticklish I couldn't bear it. There's no way I can carry you!"

Robin gave up the idea of flying—for the present, anyway—and settled for listening to Yahei talk about life.

The pigeon was very well informed. He knew all about Tatsuo Moriyama, who had left this house one day in September and still hadn't come home. Tatsuo was now locked up in a "cage" somewhere, and his wife Toko was regularly taking "feed" to him. He also told Robin that the Moriyamas' two maids had returned to their homes in the countryside, and that Toko had taken up the lawn in the garden to make a vegetable patch, planting it with autumn seedlings. Robin could see them with his own eyes. He saw that not just the Moriyamas' but all the other gardens in the neighbourhood had been planted with vegetables. Not only that, Yahei told him, but the new mound of earth in the corner of the garden was something called an air raid shelter.

Meanwhile, in the little book room, Balbo was busy making shoes. He had taken the leather cover from a magnificent black notebook, and was now making it into some lace-up shoes for Robin. It looked as though there might be enough for him to make some brogues for Fern out of it too.

"Balbo, what on earth has got into you?" she asked, puzzled. "You're obsessed with making shoes lately. Iris's red shoes, your own brown brogues, and now pairs for Robin and me."

"I'm a shoemaker by profession—it's what I do. But I must admit I do feel like I have someone on my back urging me, 'Faster! Work faster!' I don't quite understand it myself."

Balbo's hand-stitched shoes were of the highest quality, and a pair should last twenty or thirty years living in the little book room. *But still he's making new pairs for us. Even though the pair I'm wearing should last another ten or so years.* Fern had a terrible premonition. *Could it be that he's preparing for a day when we won't be able to stay in our quiet little hideaway any more?*

Trying to shake the thought from her mind, she laughed lightly and said, "Balbo, if you make new shoes for all of us, perhaps we should set up a dance club again, the way we used to!"

Memories of the large dance parties the Little People had held long ago briefly floated into Balbo's mind. During the midsummer festival, the air heavy with the scent of ripe wheat, the Little People would dance the night away, wearing out their shoes so that Balbo's grandfather and father would have their work cut out for them making shoes for some time afterwards.

Fern noticed the serene expression come over her husband's face as he was sunk in thought, as if reminiscing about the past. But it didn't last for long. He averted his eyes from her, and didn't answer.

Changes were taking place around little Yuri Moriyama, too. Her mother Toko was often out on errands to do with her father, and the maids had all left, so Yuri was kept busy with household chores after coming home from school. Coal was in short supply, and it was some time since they'd had any gas. They couldn't get hold of charcoal, either. Yuri collected firewood from the thicket in the garden. It was still too green, but once it had dried out a little, she could burn it in the charcoal stove.

She still took the daily milk—sometimes substituted with powdered milk—to Balbo and his family, who noticed how terribly chapped her hands had become.

Every time she filled the blue glass goblet with milk and took it to the Little People, Yuri recalled the stinging words of her brother Shin: *You shouldn't be doing that in these times of crisis—even soldiers don't have enough milk to drink when they fall ill.*

Was it a luxury for her to be drinking milk? And was she really wrong to give just a bit of it to the Little People, whom she loved so much? Just a tiny amount was enough to keep them alive. They were so precious to her—whenever she felt distraught thinking about her father who hadn't come back, they would quietly share in her sadness from their home on top of the bookshelf. She was determined to look after them as best she could.

But then it wasn't just her brother Shin. Yuri was in her second year at a state primary school, where she and her fellow pupils were daily exhorted to be noble children of the empire. Words like "crisis" and "unpatriotic" and "traitor" sounded darkly shameful to her.

Today was the 8th of October. Yuri and her classmates gathered at the shrine to Hachiman, the god of war and protector of Japan, to join in the school drills. The footsteps of all the pupils crunched on the gravel as they ran circuits. They all wore white headbands and ran in silence. They were not allowed to laugh or chat amongst themselves—but then, they didn't have the strength to do more than just run.

Halfway round her second lap, Yuri developed a painful stitch in her side. As she started on her third lap, she was gasping for breath and unable to speak. She felt she was about to faint, but still she pushed on to run another lap. And then, when she'd gone about half of the fourth lap, everything around her suddenly turned bright yellow and she dropped to her knees on the gravel.

When she opened her eyes a while later she was lying at the top of the stone steps to the shrine, while the rows of white headbands were still crunching their way around the circuit.

At her side stood Shin, barefoot and wearing a headband. He was the squad leader for year six.

"Moriyama!" barked the PE teacher. "Take your sister home!" His tone made it clear he despised Shin for having a weakling sister.

"Traitor!" spat Shin, his eyes narrowed.

Humiliated, Yuri stood up without his help. "I'll take myself home!"

Deep down she still believed he would come after her, but nobody followed and Shin's footsteps echoed in her ears as he took his place back in line.

When she finally reached home, her mother was on her way out of the door, dressed in baggy work pants and her arms full of bags.

"Yuri, what's up?"

"I'm not feeling well."

"They must have made you run too hard. Get your futon out and lie down for a while, will you?"

But Yuri didn't want to stay at home alone. "Are you going to see Daddy? Take me with you!"

Toko gave her a stern look. "No. It's no place for children."

How could she possibly take her daughter to see her father, who had been reduced to skin and bones in just a month inside that flea- and lice-ridden building with iron bars? Even now, when anything made of iron, from pots and pans to temple bells, had been requisitioned, that place had big iron bars. And, what's more, she didn't even know if she herself would be allowed to see him today.

She pulled herself together and quietly said, "Yuri, what would be most helpful for me would be for you to stay behind and look after the house," and left carrying a packed lunch and fresh underwear for her husband.

When Yuri turned to go back into the house after seeing her mother off, she caught sight of a grey pigeon perched on the low roof outside the little book room. As it spread its wings and flew over to the big tree, along with the loud flapping of its wings she could hear a faint flute-like sound.

Robin was on the pigeon's back! Yahei landed gently on a big branch, and Robin opened his tightly shut eyes and looked around. "I-I-I did it! I flew on the pigeon's back!"

But Yuri was feeling dizzy and feverish, and didn't notice Robin as she went back inside.

That night Balbo and the others waited and waited, but Yuri didn't come. When it got to seven-thirty, Fern took out some of the cheese she'd stored in old silver chocolate wrapping and, hiding her irritation, laid it out on the table.

"Well, everyone, let's have dinner," she said as if nothing was amiss.

What on earth could have happened to Yuri? Surely she hasn't stopped coming for good?

They were all wondering the same. But neither Balbo nor Fern said anything as they ate their cheese in silence.

The Little People were feeling how terribly dreary and cheerless dinner was without the blue glass goblet filled with milk. It wasn't just a matter of it being too dry or tasteless. The milk that little Tatsuo, Yukari and Toko, and now the new generation with Tetsu, Shin and Yuri, would leave beneath the window every day *without fail* was not just food. It was a tangible sign of their love for and devotion to the Little People, whose lives were more important to them than anything else.

Dinner was over quickly.

"I hope nothing has happened to Yuri," Balbo said finally.

"She left for school early this morning and came back home soon afterwards. She didn't look very well, and her face was very pale," added Robin, caught up in the moment.

Balbo and Fern looked at each other.

"Robin! Did you see her?" Fern's eyes were as big and round as plates.

"I, er, I just heard her footsteps and thought she sounded very weak..." he said hurriedly.

Balbo and Fern didn't say anything, but their faces showed they were thinking they would have to prepare for worse things to come.

"Robin!" said Balbo at length. "How did you get *outside?*"

I didn't just go outside, I flew on the pigeon's back!

Iris was gazing up at the air vent in the roof. Fern caught sight of the fresh chisel marks.

"Robin, you didn't!" she exclaimed loudly, clutching the hem of her apron.

Just then, they heard the sound of footsteps outside the little book room and all at once clamped their mouths shut.

It was Yuri bringing them the glass of milk on a tray, her hands trembling. She went up to the bookshelf and stood there as if petrified, lacking the strength to climb up and leave the glass of milk on the shelf under the window.

Robin moved to help her, assuming it was his role, but Fern restrained him.

More footsteps sounded outside the room, the quiet footsteps of an adult. Toko came in. Seeing Yuri there, she hurried over to her side. "Yuri, let me do that for you!"

Still in her baggy work pants, Toko climbed nimbly onto the bookshelf and picked up the blue glass goblet. Balbo and the others listened to the sound of her pouring milk into it, and watched as she placed it under the window once more.

Filled with foaming milk, as always the bright, cheerful rays of light from the blue glass made the room sparkle.

"Now then, Yuri, do you think you can sleep now? You don't need to worry any more, so you can get a good night's sleep, okay?" Toko said.

Yuri said nothing, her face expressionless.

"Yuri, please answer me. Did your teacher say anything to you this morning?"

Yuri shook her head.

"What about Shin?"

Yuri hung her head.

Toko sighed. "Well, you'd better get it off your chest now. What did he say to you?"

Haltingly, Yuri began telling her about the events at the Hachiman Shrine that morning. But as she spoke, she had the feeling that what she really wanted to talk about was something else altogether.

"Is that what happened? So you ended up coming home all by yourself!" Toko finished for her. "Yuri, it's not easy for Shin either, you know. He really believes that he's letting the country down by having a father who's been arrested and a sickly sister. He's determined to be a credit to the Japanese empire, to make up for all the other 'traitors' in the Moriyama household. He's always going on at me too, saying things like, 'You have to work harder for our country.' But you know what, Yuri? I really can't do as he says. And I can't think that either your father or the fact that you're not strong is letting the country down. And what's more, I don't think the police are right to detain your father, who hasn't done anything wrong, all this time without any investigation just because they think he has 'bad ideals'. And I can't believe that our country is right to go to war with other countries when it can't even feed its own children with a weak constitution."

She wiped the sweat from Yuri's forehead with the palm of her hand. "I'm sorry, Yuri. When you came home alone this morning, I had my head full of other things. You know your grandpa in Nojiri? I'd just heard that he was so worried about your father that he fell ill, and is in a critical condition. Grandma is old too, and I can't just leave her on her own, can I? As I was going out this morning I was hoping that they might release your father, since it's a terrible thing to lose your parents, and you can never get them back again. But the prison officers just yelled at me."

Yuri raised her eyes and looked at her mother. She had always been a bit eccentric and interesting, and had never lost her girlish quality. Now Yuri saw a thin, calm woman wearing baggy work pants. Far from having lost the youthful edge she'd always had when Daddy was at home, she hadn't been disheartened at all and was a likeable woman with her feet firmly on the ground.

"There... there's something else that's worrying me." Yuri spoke up suddenly. "Something that Shin said to me a long time ago. He said that if we have any milk, we should give it to sick soldiers. He said we shouldn't give it to *those* people, so if I'm drinking black-market milk and giving it to the Little People, doesn't that make me a traitor?"

Toko smiled irritably. "Yuri, think about it. Why shouldn't you give just a little of your own milk to people you love?" she said, holding Yuri in her characteristically fierce gaze. "Neither you nor Shin realize it, but sometimes a lot of people can be wrong. So many important people now are doing terrible things that they justify with those fine words 'for your country'—even me; if it hadn't been for Daddy, I would have been like Shin and would now be thinking of our country as something beautiful. But I realized for the first time how mistaken our country was when it locked him up because they thought he was 'dangerous'... I'm sure Daddy will be released soon, you know. But if by any chance he isn't, I won't be able to leave Tokyo. If I'm not here to take food in to him, he will die of starvation. And so, Yuri, if the day comes when children can't stay in Tokyo, I want you and Shin to go to your grandparents' house in Nojiri. And I want you to promise me that, wherever you go, you will always keep giving milk to the Little People. Will you do that for me?"

Yuri nodded fearfully.

"I can't help believing that if you can keep those vulnerable little people alive, then Daddy will be saved too... I'm sure Shin would laugh at me, though. Daddy was given the Little People and their blue glass goblet by his teacher, an Englishwoman, when he was a little boy. That alone isn't so important, but while he was looking after them and taking them their milk, something took root in his heart that affects the way he sees the world. That's why he can't agree with our country going to war, for example."

Balbo and Fern were watching Toko from the top of the bookcase as she continued speaking quietly, as much to convince herself as to encourage little Yuri.

"You know, a long time ago I read a book that told the story of how the Widow Whitgift saved the fairies, or the people of the hills as they were known. The Widow Whitgift lived in a place called Romney Marsh. Long ago, under the English King Henry VIII's reformation of the church, the people of the hills who had lived all over England since olden times ended up having to leave the country. Only one, Puck, did not give in to the sound of the church bells or the threat of the salt tide. The people of the hills loved the beautiful meadows and forests of England, and wanted to live there for ever, and their wailing echoed through Romney Marsh. The Widow Whitgift heard them, and felt terribly sorry for them. She sent her own sons to help them sail to France—and after they reached safety, they gifted the Widow and all her descendants with a strange power of sight that meant they could even see through millstones."

"Daddy has that gift too, doesn't he?" asked Yuri, remembering all the stories her father had told her when she was little.

"Well, maybe he does, maybe he doesn't. But when I read that book, I decided that if I ever got to meet anything like a fairy, I would be the sort of person to care for them. And that's what happened when I started helping Tatsuo by taking milk to the Little People."

"Tatsuo is Daddy, right?" Yuri asked shyly.

"That's right. And I can't quite explain it, but while we were taking the blue glass goblet filled with milk to the Little People, we couldn't help feeling that somehow a bond had formed between us. Our country is now at war with England, the country that Balbo's family is from. It's our enemy, but suppose Balbo and his family, thanks to your father taking them in several decades ago, turn out to be the last Little People in all the world? Isn't it terribly important we keep them alive? Over the last few decades, there have been many wars, so even the few remaining Little People hidden away in various villages and towns around the world are probably in danger of becoming extinct. So if we can get Balbo and his family safely through this, then people all over the world who care for the Little People will thank us for it, you can be sure of that."

The dark, brooding cloud cleared from Yuri's feverish face.

Oh, but I'm not even sure I can keep Tatsuo or the children safe, let alone the Little People! thought Toko as she helped Yuri back along the darkened corridor to the living room.

Meanwhile, the four Little People sat drinking the fresh milk in a convivial family atmosphere. The delay in the milk being delivered and the discovery of Robin's excursions outside were forgotten. Neither Balbo nor Fern could believe that they were the only four Little People left in the entire world.

"I've never heard of the Widow Whitgift. Our ancestors weren't so much fairies as dwarves. And they still lived in England even after that damned religious reformation," Balbo said.

"Yes, that's right," agreed Fern. "And there is always someone ready to bring us our blue glass full of milk, wherever we are." For all her natural tendency to worry, even she looked happy in the light cast by the blue glass goblet that Toko had just brought their milk in.

YAHEI THE PIGEON,
ROBIN AND THE TIGER

———

The old year came to an end, and the new year started.

In the little book room, life was getting more difficult by the day for Balbo and his family. More often than not, Yuri brought them the blue glass goblet filled with a watery concoction made from milk powder. Worried that her family were not getting the nutrition they needed, Fern sometimes supplemented their meal with a little of the cheese she had made from real milk.

During the winter, as frost flowers sparkled on the dormer window, Balbo's legs ached and he spent most of the time in bed. Iris undid one of the old woollen gloves that long ago Shin had left behind in the little book room—which Fern had squirrelled away in her storeroom—and used the wool to knit a warm cover for her father. The old yarn had lost its elasticity and kept breaking, but by binding it with some spider's silk she managed to produce a soft and fluffy camel-coloured blanket.

Robin had also become lethargic with the cold, but when spring came he got his energy back and whenever Balbo and Fern let down their guard, he would make his escape through the air vent in the ceiling.

The big tree, having lost all its leaves over winter, was now covered with a cloud of pale-green shoots, and at its foot the buds on a flowering quince had opened into white and pink shell-like blossoms. Towering over the other shrubs and plants in all the neighbouring gardens, like a lighthouse, was the spectacular white crown of the magnolia tree.

This was to be the last time Tokyo would enjoy this scene of early spring for some time, due to the imminent threat of air raids that would burn everything to the ground. Last year Robin had still known nothing of the big wide world outside, and now whenever he escaped from the little book room he could hardly believe how beautiful this view was.

Toko was overjoyed that her beloved Tatsuo, locked up in the detention centre in Nakano for being an unpatriotic liberal, had survived the winter. When she was at last allowed to meet him, Tatsuo gazed at the buds from the garden quince that she took him and gently stroked their petals. Even when Tatsuo's father in Nojiri, a mountainous area snowbound in winter, had died, soon followed by his mother, he had not been allowed out.

There was much talk of evacuating all the schoolchildren to the countryside. Yuri was now in her third year at primary school, while Shin had managed to win a place at a prefectural middle school. A high proportion of this school's students went on to join a military preparatory school for the army or the naval academy, as Shin hoped to do too.

From time to time a letter would arrive from their elder brother Tetsu, who was at school in Kyoto, asking after his father. Apparently he managed to send these letters without them being seen by the school censors, for they were full of scepticism towards the student war effort. And he often complained about the lack of food. At the end of February, Toko sent him a parcel containing some rice cakes she'd got in exchange for a kimono. It just so happened that nobody was around when it arrived and he decided to keep them all for himself, but these were hard rice cakes made from pounded glutinous rice that had to be cooked before he could eat them. He made light of this in a comical account of how, since there wasn't any fire or heating in his dormitory, he'd sneaked an electric soldering iron back to the room, but it just burned the rice cake without cooking it, and since the smell of burning would bring his classmates running he'd gobbled them down still raw with burnt patches. He also wrote emotionally about having seen off a lot of his seniors in December the previous year as they were sent to the front to die.

One day in May, Robin climbed up to the air vent and stood gazing out at the dazzling sunlight. The leaves of the big tree swayed in the refreshing breeze and the blue sky spread endlessly overhead. After the rain two or three days earlier, the sandy soil glistened like gold dust and the sweet smell of earth tickled his nose.

Robin left the protection of the rain canopy and crossed several warm roof tiles to a spot in the shade of the tree, and sat down to wait for his grey friend. Recently Yahei the pigeon had been very busy. He only showed himself for a short while on rainy days and hadn't come yesterday either, so maybe he would come today.

Honey bees were buzzing around the large blossoms of the taro plants and colourful azaleas.

"Robin!"

Hearing someone whisper his name, Robin turned round. His eyes grew big as saucers. Iris's small face was peeping out from beneath the rain canopy.

"Iris!" he stammered.

"Robin, please come and help me!" Iris said fearfully.

Robin stepped carefully over the roof tiles and went to her side.

"So I've seen *outside* too, at last! But Robin, I'm so scared I can't move."

Robin took his sister's hand and helped her sit under the rain canopy where she could gaze at the scenery in safety. Iris's little heart was beating so hard even he could hear it.

Iris hid her eyes behind her hands. Then slowly she took her hands away and gazed joyfully at the blue sky. Robin could well understand his sister's surprise.

I myself was so excited the first time! But Iris is always such a goody-goody. I wonder what made her decide to come outside?

A loud sound of flapping wings approached from afar. It must be Yahei coming in to land on a branch of the big tree.

"Iris, a friend of mine is coming. He's big, but he won't do anything bad. He's a pigeon, and his name is Yahei," he explained.

"I know," said Iris, laughing. "I've often watched you getting on his back from the dormer window. Is it fun? Robin, don't tell your friend that I'm here outside. But I want you to ask him if he's seen any other Little People like us around here. And about the bad things happening in the world outside."

She had hardly opened her mouth lately, but now her words came out in a rush. Robin stared at his sister in surprise.

Coo coo coo, called Yahei softly from the tree branch.

"You know, Robin, for some time now mother and father seem to have felt something is amiss, and they are very scared. Even so, neither of them are doing anything about it... we have to know, Robin. What is going to happen?"

Coo coo! called Yahei a little louder. As if drawn by his voice, Robin ran out from under the rain canopy.

Seeing his friend's calm and loyal figure perched on his usual branch waiting for him, Robin relaxed.

"Nice weather, isn't it?" Yahei said.

"Where have you been?" asked Robin.

Yahei looked at Robin with his thoughtful eyes and answered, "My friends moved back to the countryside yesterday—the ones who often used to come here, like Shirane and Yohei... you know, that lady pigeon with white feathers, and that grey young'un. I don't have many friends left here now."

This is my chance to ask if anything is going to happen, thought Robin.

"Yahei, is something bad about to happen? Are your friends running away from something?"

Yahei tilted his head and looked searchingly at little Robin. Then he shook his head and asked, "Don't you know? Terrible things are happening. Didn't I tell you about what happened last summer in Ueno?"

Robin shook his head and said nothing.

"I suppose you know that the humans have started a war? Since last year things have taken a turn for the worse. Food has been scarce for us, of course, and for the humans too—you must know that much. But in August last year, all the animals in Ueno Zoo were killed so that they couldn't go on the rampage if Tokyo were to be hit by an air raid—that is, if the enemy planes attack the city."

Robin knew about zoos. He had lots of friends in a zoo in the picture book.

"Was the tiger killed too?"

"Yes, the lion and tiger and leopard. Over the past two or three years, many of my friends had been living there. At least there they didn't have to worry about being shot and eaten, and there was a lot more food there than outside. But from what I heard from those pigeons, it was terrible to see the lion and tiger killed. Some of the zookeepers were against killing the animals right until the very end, but there was nothing they could do against orders given by the state. And the story of the elephant, such an intelligent animal—"

Yahei noticed Robin's lower lip trembling and stopped talking. After hearing about the tiger's death, Robin hadn't heard another word he said.

The tiger in his favourite picture book had been shot! He didn't suppose there was any undergrowth for the tiger to run around in at Ueno Zoo... it had spent all its time locked up in that small cage, and then on top of that someone had shot it... Robin covered his eyes with one arm and sobbed uncontrollably.

Yahei looked discreetly away. He couldn't bear to see his little friend so sad all of a sudden.

Finally Robin rubbed his eyes and said shyly, "I'm sorry, it's just that I used to be friends with a tiger. So—the war, is it coming closer?"

"Well, not even I know that. What I do know is that ever since last autumn when those animals were shot, rich people have been busy moving the contents of their houses to the countryside. The funny thing is that it's the big houses that are now lying empty. People call it 'evacuation'. I suppose they've started to think that it's dangerous to stay in Tokyo."

Robin thought he'd better tell Iris everything that Yahei had said, leaving nothing out. Then he remembered his sister's other question.

"Uncle Yahei, do you know of any other Little People? Have you ever come across anyone else like me?"

Yahei didn't seem to understand the meaning of his question. "We don't call moving 'evacuation'. We just say that we're moving home."

"That's not what I meant. Yahei, how many other Little People have you seen living around here?" Robin asked impatiently.

Yahei looked at him in surprise. "You're the only one I've ever met. Haven't you got any friends? Aren't you lonely?" he asked, looking a bit uncomfortable.

My sister Iris is right there, you know... but Robin kept his mouth shut. Something told him he shouldn't scare this gentle friend of his.

"You've got a mother and father, haven't you? Well, I've got a family too." Then he asked, "Have you got any children?"

Yahei flinched. "Do I look that old? I'm too young for that, I'll have you know. Although lately there hasn't been much food around, so I've got as skinny as the older birds get. My parents moved this spring to Shinshu. Now I'm left behind on my own."

Presently Yahei said goodbye to Robin and flew off to the woods around the Hachiman Shrine. He cut a lonely figure all on his own. Robin felt awful that he hadn't really given Yahei's situation much thought before now.

Yahei stayed behind in Tokyo, even though there's not enough food here, because of his friendship with me...but I never realized it!

That night, when Balbo and Fern were fast asleep in their Gelbe Sorte beds, Robin whispered to Iris. All the lights had long been turned off in the little book room, and it was pitch-black.

"Sis, are you awake?"

"Yes," Iris whispered back. When Robin told her everything he'd heard from Yahei, leaving nothing out, she sighed and said, "So there aren't any other people like us around here. Robin, I'm worried. I don't say much and am busy knitting all the time, but I'm always listening. I hear what Shin and Yuri and Toko are saying. The Moriyama family, especially Yuri and Toko, are trying to look after us. And our mother and father believe in them. But I can feel that outside there is a more terrible power than Yuri and Toko can protect us from. And so I thought we should look for other Little People to be sure we're not the only ones left in the world."

"Are we four the only ones left?" Robin whispered.

"Maybe we are, maybe we aren't," Iris said in a low voice. "But we shouldn't let that discourage us. It's great that you were brave enough to make friends with that pigeon, Robin."

"But I don't know how long Yahei will be able to stay here. If there's nothing left to eat in Tokyo, he will have to fly off to the countryside, won't he?"

Iris didn't answer.

Even after Iris's breathing had deepened in sleep, Robin remained awake for a long while. All the animals in the cute little "zoo" book that he had played with hundreds of times passed one by one before his eyes. The camel with a hump like a bunch of bananas, the lion and leopard and polar bear, the big elephant and the tiger he liked so much...

We don't want to be killed! We don't want to die! We want to live!

All the animals in the zoo opened their mouths and roared angrily. Their furious voices reverberated through him as he lay there enveloped in the darkness. Yahei the pigeon, too, had flown in from somewhere and was flapping his grey wings, shouting together with the animals.

We don't want to be killed! We don't want to die! We want to live!

Gradually, with his fists tightly clenched, he slipped into sleep.

ACORNS AREN'T FROM ZELKOVA TREES!

———

The rainy season had started early that year and was already over by the end of June, and summer arrived with July.

One day, a parcel with a Red Cross logo arrived from Toko's parents in Sydney. They had sent it via a Red Cross ship intending it to arrive in time for Christmas 1942, but it had only now reached its destination almost miraculously in July 1944. What a route it must have taken on its way to the Moriyama household!

Yuri carefully undid the string and opened it up: two packets of white sugar and half a dozen bars of soap, two cans each of sardines and corned beef, half a pound of wool (beautiful thick sky-blue wool), and half a dozen towels—and a bar of chocolate.

Yuri buried her nose in the fluffy new pure wool, saying it smelt of her grandmother in Sydney, and then in the thick starched towels that smelt of her grandfather.

"But you've never met your grandparents!" exclaimed Toko, laughing. She was stroking the string from the package to straighten out the kinks in it, tears glistening in her eyes.

Toko stowed the cans away in the cupboard for the day when Tatsuo would come home and they could sit at the dinner table as a family again. She had now grown so cautious that she believed that if she took foreign-made food to Tatsuo in prison, she could be taken for a spy.

That night, after opening the parcel, Yuri made sure to take a small amount of sugar and a piece of chocolate to the Little People, along with their milk.

The sweet taste of chocolate and sugar momentarily warmed the hearts of everyone in the Moriyama and Ashe households. Even Shin, normally so censorious, relaxed his frown when he tasted the sweet syrup spread on the salted hot cakes Yuri baked for him.

One day near the end of July, Fern had been feeling a sense of foreboding all morning.

The sugar Yuri had given them was finally running out, so she decided to bake a sweet milk cake for the family's lunch. The flour for the cake had come from some acorns that Robin had gathered outside and given to Balbo to grind into flour.

Lately they had been turning a blind eye to Robin's escapades, and he was now openly climbing through the air vent and going outside once a day. Given the wateriness of the milk Yuri was bringing them, Fern had resolved to supplement their meals with cake and so had resigned herself to him going out onto the roof to collect acorns.

She could hear Balbo grinding the acorns into flour in the next room. Having finished making new shoes for everyone in the household some time ago, he had changed his occupation to miller. He had taken an old pencil sharpener from amongst the odds and ends in Fern's storeroom and converted it to a flour mill, inserting acorns instead of pencils and turning them against the blade. He had even devised a way to adjust the blade to the diminishing size of the acorn.

"Iris!" Fern called to her daughter, who was knitting in the bedroom. As usual there was no answer. "Iris, come and give me a hand, would you?" she called again as she added the last of the sugar to the acorn flour.

Normally her daughter would appear silently at her side and help, but this time there was no sign of her.

"Iris. *Iris!*" Fern was getting annoyed.

There was a clinking noise coming from the air vent in the ceiling over the bedroom. Before long Iris appeared at her mother's side in the kitchen and without a word began kneading the flour. She poured a little of the watered-down milk into the acorn flour and deftly kneaded the mix into a dough.

Fern looked at her daughter's red-flushed cheeks. Her hair smelt of sunshine. And she was short of breath, as if she'd just run a race.

"So our little princess has become an incorrigible tomboy, has she?" she said sarcastically. "Collecting acorns is men's work. If your grandmother Beatrice Took ever saw her granddaughter climbing out through a hole in the roof..."

Iris just giggled and carried on kneading the dough, her eyes shining teasingly. Once she had finished kneading the sugared dough she took some more acorn flour, added a little salt and poured in more of the milk from the blue glass, then diligently started kneading it into another batch of dough.

"Iris! You'll give me a nervous breakdown at this rate. Are you planning to bake enough cakes to last us ten days with that amount of flour?"

Iris of course didn't answer and continued kneading with her little hands, then quickly shaped the dough into small cakes as she had been taught.

A loud flapping of wings came from outside the air vent, followed by the sound of Robin slipping quickly through the hole in the roof.

"Boy am I hungry!" he said, coming into the kitchen and putting the bag that Iris had knitted down on the floor with a thud. It was full of shiny old acorns from last year's crop. "Sis, we've got some fruit for dessert, too!"

He opened up another bag and showed them some ripe orange berries wrapped in a leaf. Fortunately he had managed to avoid squashing them.

Poor Fern went running to Balbo's worktable, her head in her hands. "Balbo, whatever has come over our children? They won't do what they're told any more! Have they lost all respect for their parents? Iris is going outside even though she's a girl, and even when I tell her off she just smiles. And then Robin rides on the back of that pigeon, of all things, and goes picking berries! It's dreadful! What if he falls off? Or if he gets attacked by another bird?"

Balbo kept his head down and carried on grinding flour. Fern buried her face in her embroidered apron and burst into tears. "It's because you spoil them that they treat us like idiots!"

From the kitchen came the sound of pancakes sizzling in the frying pan and the appetizing smell of them cooking. It was Robin's job to light the stove, using a magnifying glass to catch the sunlight.

"Fern," said Balbo quietly. "Those kids are giving things more thought than we are, you know. We're assuming that we'll go on living life as we have done up until now. It may just happen that we have to leave—"

Fern held her breath and looked at Balbo. Then she interrupted him, shouting, "No! I don't want to! Leave here? Whatever next! Forsake this quiet room to go somewhere dangerous? What are you talking about?"

"But what if this house burns down? Or what if this house gets a new owner? What will we do then?"

"If that happens, Yuri will save us! And if Yuri and the others die, then I will die along with them!" she added forlornly.

"If the children hear you saying things like that, they'll laugh at you. I myself have been thinking for some time that I've got to do something about our situation. But I just don't know what to do. It never occurred to me to go outside and ride on a pigeon's back to look around. But the children have been taking it upon themselves to find a way to do something."

Balbo stopped talking and looked at Fern. She had visibly aged over the past six months, and her pale golden hair was now streaked with white. Even though they were still living quite peacefully, the strain of making ends meet in the kitchen and coping with the anxiety of not knowing what was going to happen next had taken its toll.

Balbo gently rubbed her back as she wept, and said softly, "The pancakes are ready. How about putting a smile on and coming to have lunch? And afterwards, let's have a good talk with the children."

The dining table in the living room was set for two with one plate of delicious-looking pancakes and another of berries garnished with leaves. Just for two.

"Iris! Robin!" called Balbo, uneasily. But there was no reply.

"Balbo!" Wide-eyed, Fern looked around their home. It was shrouded in silence. Iris and Robin had gone!

She stopped crying and shook off Balbo's hand. "No, don't! Wait!" Balbo said hastily, but she ran over to the bedroom to the spot below the air vent in the roof, and started climbing frantically up.

Fern tried to ignore how much her legs were shaking inside her long skirt as she made her way up, and presently her pale face peeked out beneath the rain canopy. Almost immediately, Balbo's round face, bright red with anxiety and nerves, appeared alongside hers.

Balbo crawled to the edge of the vent and then, just as Robin had done for Iris sometime before, took Fern by the hand and helped her up, making sure she was seated safely on the ledge.

"Oh my giddy goodness, look over there!" he said.

Near the top of the big tree, on a dizzyingly high branch, was a grey pigeon. Beside it, hanging in thin air, was a hammock that sparkled in the light. It looked remarkably like Iris's handiwork, and sure enough, in it sat Iris and Robin.

Not only that, but they were in the middle of enjoying a picnic together with that grey pigeon.

"Balbo, I don't see any oak trees around here," said Fern sheepishly after a while. "How can there be any acorns on this roof?" She gazed at an oak tree in the forest around the Hachiman Shrine some distance off.

Robin and Iris, meanwhile, had noticed their parents sitting there on the ledge.

"Iris, they finally came out."

"I never thought Mother would have it in her to come out onto the roof!" said Iris, impressed.

Yahei, too, saw the two elderly Little People. "So, today's evacuation drill has been a big success, hasn't it? Now, even if there is an air raid, your parents will be able to escape," said Yahei, giving them full marks.

"It's all thanks to you, Yahei."

"Yes, it's really all your doing."

Iris and Robin fervently thanked their big friend.

After a while, and with much effort, Balbo and Fern climbed back down from the roof—going back down through the hole was a lot harder than it had been climbing up. They sat down to the dinner table and ate the sweet pancakes and fresh berries in silence.

"The children win, don't they, Balbo?" said Fern with a sigh. "They've been supporting us all this time with those acorns, and we knew nothing."

"That's enough about acorns," Balbo said shortly. "Even I realized long ago that acorns aren't from zelkova trees." He sat back down before his milling machine and resumed grinding the acorns into flour to supplement their meals.

Just the day before, Toko had been summoned to a parents' association meeting at Yuri's school to hear the head teacher talk about the upcoming mass evacuations. News of the Japanese army's crushing defeat in Saigon that July had cast a dark shadow over their lives, and now they were finalizing the plans to move all schoolchildren in groups to the countryside. Their parents had been aware of the possibility of this happening, but it still came as a shock to hear that the time had actually come to carry it out.

In homes all over the city that day, family meetings were convened and parents were deciding that, for the sake of the country, they would let their children go. Nevertheless, all those who had relations or acquaintances in the countryside resolved to send their children to them rather than as part of the group evacuation.

In the Moriyama household, too, a family meeting was held in the absence of Tatsuo and Tetsu. If the grandparents in Nojiri had still been alive, then Toko would have had no hesitation in sending Yuri to them. However, they had both passed away the previous year, and now only distant relations, two women, were living in the house.

Yuri had been allocated a place in a group evacuating to Yamanashi prefecture, but, given her poor state of health, Toko fretted over sending her to such a cold area.

"The group evacuation is just the thing for spoilt kids like you, Yuri," spat Shin. "All the other children are in high spirits looking forward to the evacuation, just like soldiers, but oh no, not you. You're such a selfish little brat!"

Shin had become even more patriotic since starting middle school, but Yuri fully understood what he was saying. Her classmates, Michiko, Yasuyo and Akiko, had been talking excitedly about how they would be able to eat white rice when they evacuated to Yamagata. She even had friends who seriously worried about not being allowed to join the evacuation if they failed the physical examination.

But Yuri, being Yuri, had only one thought on her mind. "I am not going to join the group evacuation," she declared. "I don't mind going on my own to Nojiri. But I'm not going with the group. I won't be able to take the Little People with me!"

Shin glared at her. "What kind of a reason is that? You can get Mum to look after them!"

"No. She's already too busy looking after Daddy. And anyway, I took on the responsibility of looking after them," Yuri said, unusually decisively.

Shin was getting irritated. He had been feeling increasingly angry with his little sister for placing so much importance on these English-born Little People. Since the beginning of last year, there had even been a ban on singing American and British songs. England was their enemy, but here was Yuri refusing to join the mass evacuation for the sake of those Little People. He was dying to give her a good slap.

"Shin, won't you evacuate together with Yuri?" Toko asked. "You could transfer to a middle school in Nojiri—"

"No way!" Shin said angrily. "Do you really expect me to go to some school out in the sticks? I'd never get into military prep next year if I did that. Lots of pupils from my school get accepted into the naval academy or the army because we study so hard. We get let off working in the factories because of it. Because studying for our country is more important. Yuri should join the group evacuation. If she doesn't go, she's a traitor!"

As he spoke, Shin became more and more worked up until at last he grabbed Yuri's shoulders and shook her hard.

"Behave yourself!" said Toko. "Picking on a small child, whatever next!" A bitter smile played across her lips as she contemplated this son of hers attacking his little sister on behalf of the great Japanese empire.

But this just inflamed Shin. "Shut up, Mum! You're so stupid."

He let go of Yuri's shoulders and raced upstairs.

"Mummy, quick! Don't let him—" Yuri clung onto the back of Shin's shirt as he reached the heavy door of the little book room.

On top of the bookcase, Balbo and Fern pricked up their ears at the sound of running footsteps along the corridor. The door creaked open and in poked Shin's face, twisted with hate. Behind him they could hear Yuri screaming.

"Balbo! Fern! Hide quickly!"

Iris and Robin were still outside on the roof.

"Fern, quick, there's not a moment to lose," Balbo said, grabbing her hand and pulling her towards the air vent. Last time Fern had been so frantic that she'd hardly noticed the fan in front of it, but now it seemed like an insurmountable obstacle. Nevertheless, she managed to crawl through its blades and reached the top of the vent. Balbo pushed her up from behind, then pulled himself up.

By the time Shin climbed up to the top of the bookcase and looked around the Little People's house, they had all gone.

Shin saw the fridge that he himself had made for them in the corner of the kitchen, still kept scrupulously clean although it would have been impossible to get hold of ice now. In front of Balbo's workbench, an old pencil sharpener lay on its side. Five acorns were piled up next to it.

The Little People's home was flooded with the cosy light from the familiar blue glass goblet. Seeing this, Shin's energy suddenly drained away and he slowly climbed back down off the shelf. Below, Yuri was crying, not silently as usual but wailing and sobbing hysterically.

"Where are your Little People when you need them, eh, Yuri?" Shin said as he left the little book room.

Yuri didn't know that Balbo and the others had gone outside through the air vent, but she was relieved that they'd at least managed to keep out of sight from Shin. As she'd chased after Shin into this room, Yuri had realized that she loved the Little People more than anything else. She knew now that she wasn't simply fulfilling her role as a Moriyama child—she really, truly wanted to care for them.

"Balbo, Fern! It's okay now. Iris, Robin, you can come out again now!" she called to let them know it was safe again, resolving to herself that she would look after and protect the Little People come what may.

FAREWELL, LITTLE BOOK ROOM!

Iris and Robin were relaxing in the hammock after dinner when Yahei said, "Robin, your parents are calling you."

They looked over to the roof to see Balbo and Fern outside waving at them. Unlike last time, though, this time they appeared to be in a state of panic.

"Yahei, quick, take me down to them!" Robin hastily asked his friend, and flew like the wind onto his back.

As Yahei descended to the roof, Fern and Balbo clutched onto the rain canopy for dear life, one hand outstretched like flood victims waiting for a helicopter to rescue them.

"Yahei, would you mind taking them over to the hammock?" asked Robin from his friend's back.

"No problem," said Yahei, and flew over to Balbo and Fern flapping his wings loudly. As he drew close he spread his claws as wide as he could and took hold of the pair of them. Fern screamed, but Balbo said nothing. The next moment Iris was helping her mother into the hammock, which creaked and rolled like a ship as Balbo landed in it after her. Last of all Robin jumped in from Yahei's back.

"What on earth happened?" Robin demanded.

Fern stared at her children, her face white as a sheet, unable to answer.

"Please excuse me for having taken emergency measures. You seemed to be in a terrible hurry," Yahei said to Balbo by way of apology.

Once he'd regained his composure, Balbo explained what had happened. "We heard Yuri calling out to us that it's okay to go back down now, but it was terrifying when Shin came charging into the room like that. He used to be such a sweet boy, I wonder why he's come to hate us so much. I was really convinced he might kill us."

Robin and Iris exchanged a look. They had never dreamt the crisis would come in this form. They had only lured their parents outside the last time simply to surprise them with how capable they had become.

"We can stay here for a while. Iris and I will bring food. Shin won't be able to come after us here," Robin said, trying to comfort his mother.

Yahei was eyeing a big cloud in the sky—a large cumulonimbus that appeared to be bringing rain their way.

Fern held on tight to the edge of the hammock and looked around. The very height made her feel nauseous, and she closed her eyes and said, "Balbo, I'm going back down. This place will be the death of me!"

"But listen," said Balbo fearfully, "Shin might still be down there."

"But... but I can't stand being so high up, with so much space around me. Iris, Robin, take me back down! Ask your friend to take me back."

Yahei first took Robin to check it was safe for her to return, then Iris accompanied her mother, holding onto Yahei's legs as he took them down to the roof. Balbo hadn't yet made up his mind to return. When he saw his wife and daughter were safely back inside their home, though, he bashfully asked Yahei, "I'm sorry, but would you mind taking me back too? I tend to get dizzy in high places."

He was impressed how Yahei seemed to be a loyal friend to his son. Having gently put him back down on the roof, Yahei took off once more to fetch Iris's hammock. When he came back Balbo said, "Thank you. How long have you been friends with my children?"

"Um, since last autumn, I think it was. The first time Robin got on my back, it was so ticklish I couldn't bear it! But now I hardly notice him when he rides on me," the pigeon said with a chuckle. "All the rest of my family have moved to the countryside, but I couldn't bring myself to leave Robin and Iris. Do you by any chance have plans to take your family somewhere else?"

Balbo didn't know how to answer. "I'd better ask them. I'll talk to them tonight."

The pigeon looked at him doubtfully. "Please take care. If you don't hurry up, you never know what might happen."

Balbo wiped the sweat from his brow and said goodbye to his children's clever friend.

That night, against the sound of the rain pouring outside, Balbo and his family had a meeting at Fern's bedside.

When Yuri had brought them their milk that evening, she had been deeply relieved to see they'd come back home.

"We'll probably be evacuating to Nojiri in Shinshu. Are you okay with that? You'd better start getting ready to go, okay? I'll be sure to take you with me, I promise," she told them.

The two adults in the Ashe family didn't understand what she meant by "evacuate", so Robin explained what he'd heard from Yahei, that it meant the same as "move house". He also told them about the animals in the zoo that had been killed last August because everyone expected there to be terrible air raids soon.

Fern was in bed feeling unwell. After everything that had happened today, she was a pale shadow of her usual self.

"I'll go with Yuri," put in Iris, who never normally said much. "It's dangerous to stay in Tokyo."

But however frightened Fern and Balbo were of Shin, they couldn't make up their minds to leave the quiet little book room that had been their home for so many years.

"If I end up somewhere high up, like today, or get caught in the rain, it'll be the death of me, you know," said Fern weakly, conscious of the heavy rain outside. "Everything worked out okay today because Yahei was looking out for us, but if we set out on a journey who knows what terrible things might happen..."

"When Tatsuo brought us here in a basket thirty years ago, it was terrible. We were really shaken up and down and all around. It was even worse than being in that hammock, I can tell you," Balbo said, launching into the old story.

Robin interrupted him. "Let's get one thing clear, Father. Even if you insist on staying here, Iris and I are going with Yuri. And Yahei's coming with us. We're moving to the countryside."

"Robin and Iris, wait a minute," admonished Balbo, trying to reassert his authority. "Just think—this so-called air raid might never happen. And you have to take into consideration that life in the countryside is not without its dangers..."

But Robin and Iris just shrugged. And with that, the discussion came to an end.

That night, Balbo and Fern lay awake long after the children had already fallen asleep. The faint light from their handmade lamp illuminated the bedroom. Once again they were recalling all the months and years since they had made this place their home three decades earlier. Loved by two generations of Moriyama children, they had truly been happy. They had raised two healthy children, both of them born here in Japan, and over the years had steadily acquired more furniture to make their home ever more comfortable. Until that day last year when two strange men had burst into the little book room and taken away some books, and Tatsuo Moriyama along with them, they had lived in peace.

"Why can't we just carry on living here quietly?" Fern asked Balbo.

"Why? You'll have to ask the Big People that," replied Balbo testily. "All I know is that something changed sweet Shin's heart and made him a patriot, some big, invisible force that is robbing us of our peaceful life and dragging us and the Moriyama family down into the abyss."

"But who on earth is doing such a thing?" asked Fern sharply.

"That's enough. It's late, so go to sleep," Balbo said grumpily. He himself didn't know. What on earth was that hateful force? What was its true form?

At the beginning of August, Tetsu unexpectedly came back home from Kyoto. His arrival meant they could go ahead with the evacuation of Yuri and the Ashe family right away.

The result of Yuri's physical at the end of July had meant she had officially been declared ineligible to join the mass evacuation on account of her weak bronchial tubes. Upon hearing this result, Toko began to feel reluctant even to send her to their relatives in the countryside. However, it seemed that Tetsu knew far more than Toko just how dark the prospects for the war were.

"Saipan has already fallen, and the air raids on Tokyo could start any time. Let's at least make sure Yuri's somewhere safe, Mother."

Tetsu went daily to Yuri's school and the ward office to make the arrangements for her transfer. It was decided that he would take her to Nojiri on 10th August. He also went to visit their father in prison and informed him of the plans.

Balbo and Fern had resigned themselves to the evacuation and had started making preparations for the move. Toko's foreign-made leather-covered brooch made a convenient trunk for the family's possessions, and Balbo set about removing the metal fittings.

Fern's green trunk quickly filled up with various undergarments and other clothing, as well as her sewing kit, which contained needles and thread just as it had done when she inherited it from her mother Beatrice, and the little box containing the rainbow dyes that had been passed down through generations of Little People. There wasn't enough space for her dresses, but she couldn't bear to leave them behind, and so she set about repacking the trunk.

Balbo placed the blanket that Iris had knitted for him at the bottom of his black trunk. Then he wrapped in old rags his shoemaking hammer, nails, chisel and plane, and put them on top. He greased his and Fern's new shoes before putting them in too. He intended to carry on using the mill for making acorn flour up until the morning of departure.

Iris put her rainbow-dyed spider's silk in her red Morocco leather trunk. She also put in the hammock and several skeins of the special thick, newly bleached spider's silk she used for rope. Then she neatly folded the pink silk blouse Fern had made for her a long time ago and ribbons she herself had knitted. Unwilling to be without her ivory knitting needles even for a short time, she put them in a small carrier bag she had knitted herself. Finally she squeezed in her red lace-up shoes, and with that her packing was finished.

Robin tried hard to fit his picture book into his trunk, but at 12.5 centimetres it was just too big. But he couldn't bear to part with it, since it was a memento of his friend the tiger and the other animals that had been shot at Ueno

Zoo, and so he tied it up with string so that he could carry it on his shoulders. He would hold his new lace-up shoes in his free hand.

Now that he had no use for his trunk, he decided to give it to his mother. Fern put all the emergency rations of cheese she had made over the past months into it, and then got Iris to help her prepare pancakes adapted to last them several days in the midsummer heat. They spent the 7th and 8th of August kneading acorn flour with powdered milk and frying the cakes until they were as crunchy as rice crackers, while Balbo sat at the mill grinding acorns into flour.

Yahei, upon hearing the Little People's plans to move to Shinshu, thought the time had come for him, too, to move. That spring his elderly parents and the others had left Tokyo and headed for Senkoji Temple in Nagano. It was a tough journey for the pigeons, weakened from living in Tokyo where food was scarce. But Yahei decided to go even farther north than his parents to join Iris and Robin in the vicinity of Lake Nojiri.

"I'll go on ahead," Yahei told the pair when they came out onto the roof one day. "When you get to Nojiri, tie one of Iris's colourful ribbons onto the branch of a big tree where you're living, won't you? I'll be looking out for it, so ask Yuri to tie it on a branch as high up as she can manage, okay?"

Yahei spoke calmly, but deep down he was worried whether or not he'd ever be able to find them again.

"Yahei, please take care!" said Iris, her eyes full of tears. She felt sorry that they had never been able to do anything for this big friend who had helped them so much.

"Oh Yahei, let's tie one of Iris's ribbons around your foot too. That way we can keep an eye out for you and recognize you right away," Robin said brightly.

Iris went back inside and rummaged around her rainbow-coloured ribbons in the red leather trunk, selecting the most beautiful of them to take back up to Yahei.

"Here you are, Yahei, we'll definitely see you wearing this."

"Thank you, Iris. Well, I'll be on my way."

"Goodbye Yahei!"

"Goodbye Robin!"

Yahei flew off alone north-westwards, the ribbon on his leg glinting in the light.

"Now it's just us left here."

"I do hope we'll meet Yahei again!"

The two of them sat on the branch of the big tree and watched their friend fly off until he was just a speck in the sky.

After Tetsu came home, Toko was laid up in bed for two or three days secure in the knowledge she could rely on her son to take charge.

The days passed peacefully, as if the war and all it involved were far away. Once she had recovered, she made some new indigo-dyed work pants and an extra air raid hood for Yuri. When she had finished those, even though the weather now was hot she took out some wool and started knitting a jumper for her daughter. She had hardly ever met the two women at the house in Nojiri, and though they were relatives she was still a little reluctant to entrust her sickly daughter to them. For the moment, though, it made her feel better to be busying herself with knitting something for her with the wool her grandparents in Sydney had sent.

Yuri found a big rattan basket in her father's bedroom. It was apparently what he'd used to bring Balbo and his family to this house all those years ago, and so she spread out her own baby blanket inside it, and covered this with one of the towels that had come from Sydney. This would be the Little People's home while they were travelling in the train. Once she had added their own trunks and the blue glass goblet, the Little People's preparations for the move would be complete.

On the evening of 8th August, Tetsu queued up at the station to buy their tickets. Yuri joined the crowds waving off her school friends joining the mass evacuation, as if they were soldiers being sent off to fight. When she saw Yasuko and Kumiko and the others in such high spirits, as if they were off on an excursion, she felt a bit lonely at being the odd one out. But once they arrived at the darkened Ueno Station and the schoolchildren went alone onto the platform, even Yasuko and Kumiko's eyes filled with tears. And Yasuko's mother, who took Yuri home afterwards, cried all the way back. Yuri clutched tightly onto her hand, but her thoughts were filled with her impending separation from her own mother, and couldn't think of anything to say to comfort her.

If there was anything that worried Yuri about going to Nojiri, it was that she had to leave without patching things up with Shin, and without being able to see her father.

For some time now, whenever Yuri mentioned her father, her mother's face would freeze and the atmosphere would suddenly feel tense. And so she would hold her tongue as surely as if someone had hissed "Shhh!" In her dreams, though, her father always looked skinny and covered in blood like the picture of Christ on the Cross that she'd seen in the little book room. And he was saying something to her, but she couldn't hear what. However much she called *Daddy, Daddy!* she couldn't hear his answer.

On 9th August, Toko came to Yuri's room dressed in her best black work trousers.

"Yuri, get dressed and let's go. We're going to see your father."

Yuri looked at her mother in surprise.

"Can you promise me that whatever you see, you won't ask questions, and you won't cry?"

Yuri nodded and stood up.

They had to change trains several times before arriving at the grey building where her father was imprisoned. She and her mother entered through a door with iron gratings. The loud clang as it slammed closed behind them was followed by the heavy clunk of a key turning in the lock.

And there, standing right in the middle of the room, was her father. He wasn't covered in blood as in her dreams. But his gentle, indulgently good-humoured face had become horrifyingly bloated and was covered with a beard, and she realized how much he had been suffering.

"When you go to Nojiri, I want you to become as suntanned and strong as the local children." Then, saying nothing more, he sat smiling at her with infinite gentleness.

In this hot, oppressive room Yuri felt exhaustion seep through her body and thought she might suffocate from the heat and shock. The fact that her father could smile at her so gently was almost more than she could bear.

At last the grey door opened once more, and they heard the clunk of the lock being turned behind them as they left the building in which her father was imprisoned and went outside again.

But why? Why on earth? Yuri suppressed the questions that rose to her lips as she walked alongside her mother. Even if she never got to meet her father again as long as she lived, she would never forget that smiling face he showed her today, she thought.

The night of 9th August was a sleepless one, both for the Moriyama family and the Ashe family. Toko was up until nearly one o'clock finishing off Yuri's sweater. At the beginning of last year, grown-up Tetsu had left home, then Tatsuo had been taken away, and now little Yuri was about to leave... Toko couldn't shake the idea that her family was being broken up. In just one or two years, some great force had risen up and trampled on her wishes and forcefully scattered all the members of the happy family she held so dear. No, it wasn't just the Moriyama family—parents and children in families all over Japan had been robbed of the happiness of living together.

Tetsu and Shin tossed and turned in bed, apparently unable to sleep. Yuri slept, utterly worn out. Toko focused on her knitting, thinking that she didn't want to lose any of these children.

In the little book room, too, the two children were asleep but Fern and Balbo lay awake. Just the thought that this was their last night in the Gelbe Sorte beds they had used for the past thirty years was enough for Fern to choke up.

"We'll be able to come back here, won't we?" she pressed Balbo.

"Let's hope so," he replied, his voice tremulous.

81

It was nearly dawn by the time they managed to sleep. The lamp in their room used up the last remaining oil and fizzled out.

Day broke on 10th August.

Toko cooked up some special red-bean rice, using precious white rice with azuki beans, for Tetsu and Yuri to take with them for the journey.

Thanks to Tetsu's cheerful presence, the morning of Yuri's departure was a lively occasion. Shin completely ignored the preparations for the Little People but Tetsu helped Yuri take the big old basket up to the little book room.

Iris and Balbo had come halfway down the bookshelf and were waiting for them. Tetsu felt his chest tighten upon meeting them after such a long, long time. Balbo had visibly aged, while Iris had grown into a beautiful young woman. Neither showed any hesitation as they stepped fearlessly onto the palm of his hand. Gently, Tetsu carried each of them, together with their luggage, to the basket.

In the little home up near the ceiling, he could hear a sound like bumble-bee wings. It was Fern and Robin arguing. It had been so long since he'd heard the Little People's voices that he had lost the ability to distinguish between them. And so he climbed up the bookcase and peered in at them. The little boy was staggering under the weight of a book as big as himself that he was attempting to hoist onto his shoulders. His mother was trying to stop him, telling him it was dangerous.

Tetsu deftly took the book from him. It was old, and had the title *The Zoo* printed on its yellow cover. Tetsu had never seen it before. He gestured to the boy that he would put it in the basket for him. Overjoyed, Robin carried his own black lace-up shoes and his mother's trunk onto Tetsu's outstretched hand.

Fern was the only one left, but she was clearly terrified of Tetsu. Now in his second year of high school, he was 170 centimetres tall, and a fine young man. It was hardly surprising that Fern, at barely 14 centimetres, was scared of him.

Noticing this, Yuri went to her rescue. Keeping her eyes firmly shut, Fern stepped onto Yuri's hand. Balbo and the others were waiting anxiously as Yuri gently placed her in the bottom of the basket with them. Once she saw that they were all safely settled in Fern shrieked, "The fridge! My fridge!"

Yuri asked Tetsu to get the fridge from the Little People's kitchen and he put it into the basket with them, along with the mysterious blue glass goblet and a can of precious milk powder. Now they were ready for the move.

"Everyone okay? Be patient now. When we reach the house in the mountains this evening, I'll make your home right away," Yuri told them kindly.

The basket's lid creaked as she lowered it and snapped the clasp shut. It wobbled as she lifted it up, and Fern closed her eyes tightly.

"Farewell! Farewell!" Robin and Iris poked their arms through the gaps in the basket and waved to the little book room that had been their home. The dust-covered books remained silent as always.

"Goodbye!" Yuri, too, as she stepped out of the little book room turned back for one last look. It was the same as always, with the morning light glittering green and gold as it filtered down through the leaves of the big tree outside.

*   *   *

Yuri and Tetsu headed for Ueno Station accompanied by their mother and Shin. Tetsu had a rucksack on his back, while Yuri carried the basket with the Little People, now quiet, inside. Toko was carrying Yuri's case, which contained the sky-blue jumper that she'd just finished knitting for her that morning.

How much more cheerful it was to set out in the morning than it had been for the mass evacuation that had left at night! When at last they arrived at the station, they found it thronged with people and luggage and flags and banners. Here and there they heard groups cheering *Banzai!* as they saw off soldiers on their way to the front.

"Well, it's time for you to go. Take care now!"

"See you again soon!"

With barely time for a proper farewell, Yuri left her mother at the ticket gate and concentrated on joining the throng of people headed for the platform. With his free hand, Tetsu held tightly onto her and pulled her along with him. With her heart pounding, and jostled this way and that among the large pieces of baggage, she at last managed to push her way onto the train and get safely seated.

The train quickly filled up, with people occupying every available space in the aisles and bathrooms, and even on the floor at Yuri's and Tetsu's feet. They were all terrifying, with menacing looks on their faces.

"Yuri!" Tetsu shook her shoulder and pointed to the window. Yuri peered outside through all the people. On the commuter train platform next to theirs stood Toko and Shin.

"Yuri! Hey, give them a wave!" Tetsu pushed his little sister, who was sitting in a daze, closer to the window.

Shin noticed her and pointed her out to Toko, who was holding a handkerchief to her eyes. Shin bit his lip and stared at Yuri with wide-open eyes. Tears dripped from Yuri's eyes onto the basket on her lap. Tetsu pushed in front of her again and, waving, shouted something out of the window.

The train started moving off, to a chorus of *Banzai!*

Shin was waving now, his face pale.

"Goodbye!"

Yuri was quite unable to move and she sat gripping the basket on her lap, the tears streaming from her eyes.

THE HOUSE IN THE MOUNTAINS

———

*C*lickety clackety claaaang!

The train shuddered to a halt. Densely forested hillsides pressed in on either side of the tracks, and a river flowed noisily nearby.

Shaken out of sleep, the passengers started clamouring. The train had almost reached Furuma, the stop before Tetsu's and Yuri's station. Everyone waited in their seats, but as time passed without them knowing what the problem was, they began to grow restless.

A ruckus broke out in the carriage before theirs and people started jumping out onto the tracks. A railway official approached and informed them that a little up ahead a freight train had been derailed, and the tracks were impassable in both directions. Nobody could tell how long it might take to put things right, he added, as he headed for the next carriage. All around them, the soldiers wearing red sashes across their chests—signifying they were headed for the front—paled and became agitated. Stepping over the people in the aisle, they clustered on the platform between the carriages discussing something excitedly.

Tetsu agilely climbed out of the window and down onto the tracks, and went to take a look up ahead. The red-sash-wearers jostled with each other as they jumped down from the platform and then set off at a run as if something was after them.

After a while Tetsu came back and told her, "Yuri, we'll have to walk." Once they made it to Furuma, they would probably be able to hitch a ride with a truck to their station at Kashiwabara. And trains were apparently running from there, he told the other passengers in their carriage.

Yuri was actually quite relieved to get out of the train, which was far too hot. It felt pleasant to breathe in the cool, dry air outside, where they could hear the river.

"Are you okay walking?" asked Tetsu as he hoisted his ruck-sack onto his back and picked up Yuri's heavy case. As well as the basket, Yuri was carrying an air raid pack and the remains of their lunch.

"I'm fine," Yuri said, and smiled.

All the passengers started walking along the tracks, carrying their luggage like refugees. Elderly women tied hand towels around their heads as protection against the afternoon sun, while mothers pulled their children along by the hand as they made their way towards the next station.

As they passed the pitiful scene of the overturned freight

train and broken tracks and entered the dark tunnel, Yuri gulped and tried to hide her tears from Tetsu, who was leading her by the hand. Her feet were beginning to hurt, and though she was doing her best to be brave she was feeling anxious and beginning to miss her mother.

The light of a single torch came from behind to illuminate the ground beneath their feet. Yuri swallowed her tears and looked at the person lighting the way for her. A young woman wearing trousers was walking at her side.

As they neared the end of the tunnel and could see the bright sunlight, the woman turned off the torch and walked quickly on ahead without giving either Yuri or Tetsu a chance to thank her. A rucksack swung heavily on her back. They couldn't tell whether she was a local or whether, like them, she was from the city.

An army truck was parked on the road alongside the tracks near Furuma Station. It picked up people with a pass certifying they were on official military business, soldiers headed for the front, or civilians being drafted in for army work, and drove off in a cloud of dust.

"Damn!" muttered Tetsu, and stared at the dusty white road.

Yuri looked pleadingly at her brother. She herself was exhausted, but she was even more worried about the Little People in the basket. Had they survived being shaken around non-stop since morning?

Tetsu fully understood his little sister's concern. "Yuri, it doesn't look like we'll be able to get a lift in a truck after all, so shall we take the mountain path to the lake? I've been that way from Furuma before, and I think we'll be able to reach the house before dark."

A steady stream of people passed by them, apparently resigned to walking to the next station at Kashiwabara. Yuri agreed it would be better to take the mountain path, where she could let the Little People breathe fresh air out of sight of the crowd. It was about three-thirty. Had it not been for the accident, they would almost be at their grandparents' house by now.

Tetsu hoisted Yuri's case onto one shoulder and set off up the mountain path. He was dripping sweat and the straps of his rucksack dug into his shoulders, and though the path wasn't all that steep his heart pounded. He knew that his little sister had been crying in the tunnel earlier. This was what war meant, he thought with a frown: not allowing such a small girl to travel in the truck just because it was meant for the war effort; a young girl walking along hiding her sadness at leaving her mother; so many women and children walking uncomplainingly along the tracks...

The baggage me and Yuri are carrying on our backs is like that monstrous Old Man of the Sea, *the one that the sailor in the* Arabian Nights *couldn't get rid of. I've accepted that, and I'm even trying to beautify it as something heroic, a burden of war—but is that right? What if ten years from now I find out it was a big mistake? No, that'll never happen. I'll be sent off to the front to kill the enemy and die for my country long before then.* Tetsu recalled the words of one of his school friends in Kyoto: *Our life as students is just a stay of execution—just until we go to war and die.* He shook off the sweat that was running down into his eyes.

White as a sheet, Yuri walked behind her brother. Everything around her looked yellow, perhaps because of her usual anaemia. Soon they were walking in long grass. Here and there pale purple bellflowers sparkled, and cream-coloured daylilies trembled.

Young pampas grasses higher than an adult's shoulder stretched out their pretty leaves. They emerged above the tree line onto the gentle slopes of a highland plain, and heard the call of a bush warbler from below.

"Yuri, we just have one more mountain to cross and then we'll see the lake!"

Tetsu threw his rucksack onto the grass and flopped down on his back. Yuri gently put the basket down and then sat beside it. Immediately, black flies came and bit their bare arms as if they'd been lying in wait.

They heard the grass behind them rustle, and then a white goat appeared, followed by a suntanned woman dressed in trousers. Yuri seemed less surprised than the woman herself, who exclaimed, "Are you two going to the lake too?"

Discreetly closing the clasp on the basket, Yuri nodded. Tetsu sat up abruptly, startling the goat.

"Stop it now, behave yourself," the woman told it, and started walking away.

Wasn't she the one who had shone the light at their feet in the tunnel? She didn't seem all that accustomed to dealing with goats, as the animal was fairly dragging her along.

"We're going to Tsuchigasaki, and from there passing below Kamiyama," Tetsu said to her departing figure, almost as if to himself.

The woman turned and said, "You'd better hurry up, then. The sun'll be going down soon."

Tetsu looked at his watch and stood up hurriedly. Without a word, Yuri picked up the basket and followed after her brother.

Carrying her rucksack and holding onto the goat's lead, the woman pushed her way through pampas grass taller than herself and climbed steadily up. Tetsu shifted Yuri's case from his right shoulder to the left, and struggled to keep up with her.

As they reached the top of the pine-forested hill, they at last glimpsed the quiet blue of Lake Nojiri stretching as far as they could see. The white goat set off down a narrow path through the pine forest towards the lake, and the woman followed after it as nimbly as a mountain serow.

"Come on Yuri, we'd better hurry too!"

Tetsu seemed to have forgotten his tiredness and went bounding down the steep slope towards the lake. Yuri watched as he caught up with the woman and the two of them stood on the path talking about something. She wasn't used to the mountain path and nervously picked her way down step by step.

"Yuri, give me the glass. She'll give us a little milk," called Tetsu while she was still some way off.

Yuri came to herself with a start and put the basket down on the slope before gently opening the lid and feeling around for the glass.

"I'm not used to milking. I've been trying to get hold of a goat for some time and today I finally managed to persuade an acquaintance in a farmhouse in Furuma to let me have this one," the woman said as she nervously pulled at the goat's teats. Yuri watched as pure white milk spurted into the glass, filling it about halfway.

"I'm sorry, that's about all I can get from it," said the woman, embarrassed.

Yuri thanked her and took the glass, and casually went back to the basket. The woman led the goat on and went to wash her hands in the lake.

*   *   *

Inside the basket, Robin breathed the fresh air that came flowing in and opened his eyes. With the hot, humid weather and the incessant jolting of the train, the Little People had become so tired they had fallen into a deep sleep. And Robin had only just noticed now that Tetsu and Yuri had left the train and started walking.

The lid of the basket rose a fraction and Yuri's hand slipped in and took the blue glass goblet. A short while after, she slipped it back half full of fresh warm milk.

"Robin! Iris! Get everyone to drink it quickly—we don't have much time," she whispered urgently. Her face was smeared with soot and looked very pale.

Robin hurriedly shook his parents awake and they took turns moistening their parched throats with the most delicious milk they had tasted for a long time.

"It's goat's milk!" whispered Balbo.

"It's frothy!" added Iris.

"Oh, I can feel myself coming back to life," said Fern, regaining her energy. "It's like I've been hovering between life and death all this time!"

They heard the sound of footsteps on dry twigs approaching, and suddenly Yuri hissed: "Shhh!"

The silence of the mountainside was broken only by the cheerful chirping of a bush warbler, before they heard the voice of an unknown woman ask, "Is your sister feeling a little better now?"

"Yuri, was the goat's milk good?" That was Tetsu's voice.

"Very!" replied Yuri, and with that the basket was suddenly lifted into the air.

Through the gaps in the basket, Robin could see a vast blue

expanse of water. A refreshing breeze was blowing up from its surface lightly rustling everything around them.

"Well then, let's be on our way," Tetsu said to his sister and, hitching his rucksack higher on his shoulders, he set off. The woman and a white animal that Robin had never seen before—the goat that had just supplied their milk—followed after him.

Robin's eyes grew wide as he took in the landscape around them. They were in the mountains. Green trees that Robin had never seen in his life grew thickly all around. He breathed in the invigorating smell of resin, and felt as if the greenness was seeping all the way down to the bottom of his lungs.

As soon as the basket began moving again Balbo, Fern and Iris buried their faces in the towel with their eyes shut tight, but Robin kept his eyes firmly open. And for the next two hours he watched as they made their way along the lakeside path. The Big People walked on in silence, stepping over the black earth covered in dry leaves, past all the holiday homes left empty by their foreign owners, and listening to the waves lapping at the water's edge.

As the big red sun sank gradually below the far shore of the lake, Tetsu and Yuri took their leave of the woman and her goat and turned off onto a mountain path. Soon after cutting through a larch forest, they entered the kitchen of a farmhouse filled with the fragrance of a wood fire.

The Little People's new home was to be a shelf near the ceiling of a room inside this straw-thatched cottage surrounded by potato fields. The evening they arrived, and for the next couple of days, they stayed in the safety of the basket with bated breath, venturing out only to fetch the milk that Yuri left for them by the window.

There were just two Big People in this house, a woman with a no-nonsense voice and her quiet, elderly mother, with none of the rowdy children that Fern had feared might be there. She was also relieved to note that, just as in the little book room, there didn't seem to be any sign of mice—or worse, cats.

That first evening Fern and Balbo had been so worn out that they slept dead to the world, but on the second night Fern complained that she couldn't sleep because of the *tick tock tick tock* of the big grandfather clock.

The next morning Balbo peeped through the cracks in the basket at the clock, which stood right before them.

"Goodness gracious me, I've seen a clock like that somewhere before." It was an old-fashioned grandfather clock with the pendulum swinging in its case below the big round gold-rimmed face. "Maybe it was in Miss MacLachlan's house... or was it in the Moriyama house that we saw one?" he whispered to Fern.

This particular clock was English-made. Tatsuo Moriyama's father had bought it long ago at an international exhibition in the Meiji period, and had grown so used to it that, when he retired here from Tokyo, he brought it with him and stood it against the wall in the living room. However, Balbo and Fern couldn't possibly have seen it before. In all their thirty years in the Moriyama house, they had not once entered the living room there.

"Still, it makes me come over all nostalgic, it does... Just think, it must have crossed the sea sometime to reach Japan," muttered Balbo fondly as he gazed at the name "Birmingham" at the bottom of the clock face. Robin clung onto his father's back and looked at the clock with him. Balbo gestured at him to keep quiet.

There was the sound of feet shuffling over the *tatami* towards them, and a woman opened the door to the room. A sweet old lady with white hair and a round face appeared quietly in the doorway. With her eyes still closed, she made her way over to the clock and fumbled with her hands to open the door for the pendulum case. Taking out the gold key from behind the pendulum, she began winding up the clock.

Balbo and Robin watched her in silence. The poor woman was blind. Robin had never seen a blind person before, and he timidly hid behind Balbo's back. Once she finished winding up the clock, the old lady listened to confirm the *tick tock* then shuffled back out of the room.

"She's probably got sharp hearing. We must be careful not to speak in loud voices," Balbo whispered to the others.

Once they realized that the only Big Person who ever came into this room was the blind old lady, the Little People were relieved. Ever since they had left the little book room, they had felt as anxious as a snail without its shell. They had always enjoyed the peace of mind afforded by the constant silence of the little book room and the fact that strangers never entered there, but in this house in the countryside they never knew when someone might come in, and they felt exposed and constantly anxious that they might be seen.

On the morning of the third day, Tetsu came into the room with Yuri, who had black bags under her eyes and was visibly thinner.

"Well then, let's make the Little People's new home, shall we?" said Tetsu brightly. Then he stepped up onto an old chest and peeked at the shelf up by the ceiling. "Wow, it's covered in soot here!"

He lifted down the basket with Balbo and the others in it and placed it on the *tatami* for the moment. He cleaned the shelf, then took some of his grandfather's old books and used them to block off the right corner of the shelf, then he took a small box made of paulownia wood and a cardboard box from his grandfather's desk and put them together on the shelf to make a new house for Balbo's family.

"Yuri, where do you want to put the blue glass goblet?" he asked his little sister.

"How about by the window here?" she said, pointing at the lattice window where she had been placing the glass for the last couple of days.

Hanging by the window was a sedge hat that had probably belonged to their late grandfather. If she put the glass behind it, the Little People would be able to come and collect it from the end of the shelf without being seen by anybody. Tetsu checked the window to make sure the glass of milk couldn't fall out of it or be knocked over whenever it was opened or closed.

"So, we're all set then. I'll put the chest under the window so that you can reach the sill more easily, Yuri," Tetsu said. "The house is a bit shabby, but I think they'll be safe here." He put the Little People's basket on the shelf, opened the lid and laid it on its side so they could get out easily.

"Well then, hurry and finish moving while we keep watch outside the door!" Yuri told them, and went out of the room with Tetsu.

The blind old lady, whom Yuri called Granny Oto, was sitting on the veranda grinding some buckwheat flour in a stone mortar for

Tetsu to take back to Tokyo with him that night. Her daughter, whom Yuri called Aunt Toyo, was Tatsuo and Toko Moriyama's cousin. She had already gone out to the mountainside fields early that morning, and so for the first time since they had arrived at this house, Tetsu and Yuri were at last left alone and could finish the Little People's move.

"You'll be starting school soon and can make new friends," said Tetsu, deliberately nonchalant. In reality, he knew very well that it wouldn't be easy for Yuri to fit in with life here in the countryside.

Little Yuri's arrival at the home of the two women, with no man about the house, simply meant another mouth to feed in a household where food was already in pitifully short supply. It wasn't just the food. Collecting firewood, drawing water from the well—everything had to include one more person, Aunt Toyo had explained to Tetsu. Although she was about the same age as Tetsu's and Yuri's parents, her hair was completely white and her front teeth were missing, and she looked much older than her years.

In Tokyo, even though everything was in short supply, Toko could still sometimes get hold of butter or sugar and they at least could scrape by. But here in the countryside, they had to do all the work themselves just to eke out what in Tokyo were considered the basics. There was very little to eat other than rice and potato porridge, or boiled barley and rice, and Aunt Toyo had to work hard just to produce that much. Even Granny Oto toiled the whole day grinding up flour and twisting straw into rope. Yuri wouldn't be able to lead the pampered life of a city child here.

"The powdered milk won't last until winter," said Yuri,

worried as usual about the Little People. "I wonder if I'll be able to get that woman with the goat to give me some milk?"

"That goat doesn't just belong to her, you know," Tetsu replied. "She shares it with some friends. I went to see her yesterday, thinking she might let you have some milk. She's called Katsuko, by the way, and she lives in a village called Hondo. She used to come to Nojiri every summer with other women in her working women's club, and five or six of them were evacuated here in the spring of 1943 and are running a proper farm. They said that after the snow melted this spring they ploughed the fields and planted rice for the first time."

"Is that far from here?" Yuri asked, listening to the faint rustling of the Little People as they moved their belongings into their new home.

"If you carry on past your school and walk about an hour up the valley, you'll come to a secluded village with about five or six houses. That's where they live. In the busy farming season they run a crèche and a club for children, and put on *kamishibai* picture-card plays like 'Let's be sure to put away our bedding', and 'Let's be sure to dry the chopping board', and try really hard to make themselves useful to local people."

Tetsu suddenly stood up and took out a small wrap of paper from the rucksack he had brought with him. "Yuri, I bought this in Tokyo for you. Look, it's sparklers. When I went to the toy shop this was all they had left. I was thinking we could enjoy them together when I leave tonight, but let's keep half of them for those women. They could probably use things like this for their children's club."

Yuri suddenly remembered that her brother was about to leave, and couldn't answer right away. Tetsu pressed the packet of sparklers into her hand and went out into the garden where Granny Oto sat on the sunny veranda grinding flour.

"Before I leave I'm going to the mountains to collect your share of firewood for the coming winter, Yuri!"

"Wait! Take me with you! Even I can carry firewood."

Yuri checked that the Little People were settled in on the shelf, then followed Tetsu outside.

A DAY OF GRASS-CUTTING

—

After Tetsu's departure, Aunt Toyo's house in the shade of the forest returned to its customary silence.

Every day, Yuri followed her hard-working aunt into the mountains to collect firewood. She got her to help secure the heavy bundle to her back, and then, as she came back down the mountain path, her light body gained momentum and she was able to descend the slope in one go. On the way her knees wobbled and chest pounded and she thought she would never make it, but she was surprised that her strength held up all the way to the bottom.

Aunt Toyo realized that the reason city-bred Yuri was following her around all day was probably that she was missing her mother, and didn't let on how much of a burden she was to her.

But the truth was that Yuri was too frightened of Granny Oto to stay at home with her all day. She felt sorry for the old woman being blind, but she just couldn't help being scared of her. The empty farmhouse was dark even in the afternoon, and when the quiet old woman stood in silence by the sunken hearth, Yuri felt all the hairs rise up on the nape of her neck. However wrong she knew she was, being alone in that house where the sun barely reached filled her with indescribable terror.

From time to time a letter from Toko in Tokyo would arrive in a long white envelope. In her replies, Yuri would criticize herself for being scared of Granny Oto. She knew that her mother would probably take Granny Oto to a sunny spot outside, or into the pleasant woods, and sit her where there was plentiful fresh air, but the moment she herself tried approaching the unseeing old woman she would flinch and back away again.

September came round and Yuri started attending the school by the lake. It took her about twenty minutes to get there on foot. She couldn't help feeling relieved at being able to get away from the two women during the day, and while some of the children at school bullied her for being the "pale kid" or the "evacuee", others were exceptionally kind to her.

Two days every week the children from her school would do voluntary work at various farms in the area. At the beginning of September the younger children like Yuri were set to cutting grass. The farm kids brought their own sickles that they had sharpened themselves, while Yuri and some others had to borrow theirs from the school. They would each hoist a wooden frame onto their back, and set off for the farm.

Yuri looked forward to the grass-cutting. She was always thinking that in order to find milk for Balbo and his family, she had to get to know farmers who kept a cow or a goat. Also, whenever they went grass-cutting they would always receive some treat from the farmhouse—steamed buns containing wheat bran, or freshly steamed sweet potatoes. In Aunt Toyo's house they ate whatever they had available, and when there was, say, pumpkin then they would have pumpkin for dinner several days running. However, the better-off farmhouses liked to treat the pupils who went to work for them.

"Your Korean shoes are great!" a big boy called Tsutomu told Yuri.

This was what the village kids called the simple rubber plimsolls that fit on either foot which schoolchildren in Tokyo were given on rations. Yuri compared her friend's large, sunburnt feet in straw sandals with her own narrow feet in plimsolls and laughed.

That morning, they were going to work for a farmer called Isoguchi in Hondo. By September Nojiri was already well into autumn. The ripples on the blue lake sparkled, while Mounts Kurohime and Iizuna looked close in the crisp air and golden light.

Recalling that Hondo was the name of the village where Tetsu had told her Katsuko was living, Yuri looked forward even more than usual to the grass-cutting. As they climbed up the mountain path, Yuri turned round again and again to gaze at the lake. She looked so cheerful that Tsutomu, the boy who had teased her about her plimsolls earlier, felt half relieved and half sorrowful.

Last month he had heard that a girl evacuee was in Toyo Moriyama's house, and so he had gone to see for himself. When he reached the pass overlooking the lake, thunderclouds billowing up over Mount Kurohime were surrounded by smaller puffs of cloud that looked like a shoal of goldfish, dyed red by the setting sun.

A little girl was crouched there on a stone gazing in silence at the sunset. She looked frail, and reminded him of a newly hatched pond smelt. Tears were streaming down her face, and he had the impression she had been saving them up for when no one else was around to see them. He was struck by how much this little girl from Tokyo must miss her mother. Suddenly he, too, had felt the urge to cry and, careful not to make a sound stepping over the dry twigs, he turned to go back home.

He had assumed that the little girl would be entering year one, and was half annoyed and half amused when Yuri Moriyama joined his year-three class in the new term. He teased her more than anyone else did, and was sometimes nasty to her too, but he felt somehow relieved to see the cheerful smile on her face, now suntanned so that she was no longer the "pale kid".

After climbing over several hills, Yuri and her classmates finally gazed down upon Hondo, a cluster of straw-thatched cottages huddled in amongst the paddies of ripening yellow rice.

They spread out over the mountainside and began cutting the grass. A strong herbal fragrance of mountain and pampas grasses wafted up around them. But however hard Yuri worked, her pile of cut grass was never as high as the other children's. Once Tsutomu and Keiko had finished their own spots, they went over to help her, rapidly bringing her pile up to size.

At last the children piled the cut grass onto the wooden frames they carried on their backs, and made their way down the steep path in single file, Yuri's head bobbing as she ran to keep up with them. Once they gained momentum it was impossible to stop, however tough it was to keep going, and Yuri was thankful for her "Korean shoes", which really helped to protect her feet from stones and tree roots.

Upon reaching the Isoguchis' house they were met by five or six women, who took the cut grass from them and stored it away inside a big barn. Just like on the other farms in the area, all the young men had gone off to war. As the children rested in the garden by the veranda, the women brought out some paper-wrapped boxes for them. They looked just like the box of sweets that Yuri was given at the inaugural ceremony at her primary school. At most farmhouses the children were given steamed buns or sweet potatoes as they were, not in any wrapping, so these boxes were quite unusual. And among the women, Yuri recognized Katsuko.

"Oh, wow! It's white bread!"

"It's sweet!"

Unlike the girls, who were rather shy, Tsutomu and the other boys immediately ripped off the paper and began eating. Each package contained steamed buns made with goat's milk and sweets shaped like camellia flowers made from steamed sweet potatoes.

When Yuri opened up her package and saw the pinkish flower-shaped sweets inside, her eyes suddenly felt hot. Without realizing it, this was just what she had been craving—and now it was suddenly there before her. After the food shortages began, for birthdays and special occasions her mother Toko would squeeze sweet-potato pulp through a cloth to form flower-shaped sweets for her. In Aunt Toyo's household, however, they were all far too busy to do anything like that. However dull the food was in Tokyo, Yuri's mother had always made an effort to make it as tasty as possible. A silent tear dropped onto the pink camellia in her hands.

"Tasty, eh? The lasses from Tokyo made 'em for us," old Grandpa Isoguchi told the children, who had fallen quiet when they saw this unusual food. Local people didn't have much good to say about Grandpa Isoguchi, who rented out the fields to the young women evacuees, but he clearly enjoyed surprising the village kids with such unusual handmade delicacies.

Yuri slowly savoured the tasty treats, and ate just one of the steamed goat's milk buns. She decided to take the flower-shaped sweet back for Granny Oto and the other steamed bun to Balbo and his family.

As the school party got ready to go back home, Katsuko came up to Yuri. "You're Moriyama's little sister, right? How is your brother?"

Yuri nodded, saying nothing. She hadn't received any letter from Tetsu, but she'd just recently had a letter from Toko telling her that he was doing fine in Kyoto.

"Have you got used to school now? Your brother was really worried about you, you know."

In the end, Yuri said goodbye to Katsuko without telling her that she had some sparklers from Tetsu for her, or asking if she could come and get some milk from her from time to time.

On the way back, the children couldn't resist taking out the remaining white buns and flower-shaped sweets from the parcels and eating them all up. The young woman teacher with them pretended not to notice.

Yuri was determined not to eat the contents of her package that she had saved for the others at home. But she hadn't tasted milk for so long, and her resolve began to weaken. She resisted the temptation longer than most, but eventually she gave in and ate the flower sweet. And just as they were getting close to school and the blue lake came into view, she ate the milk bun that she had been saving for the Little People.

In the Little People's home, Fern was hurriedly doing some needlework as she listened to the *tick tock* of the old grandfather clock. The mountain air was growing cold, and even wearing all their clothes they still felt the chill.

"It's going to be terribly cold this winter. I can feel it in my knees," said Balbo, looking worried.

"That's why I'm making you another quilt." Fern had opened out the roll of fabric scraps she'd brought from Tokyo and was using them to stitch together a patchwork quilt cover.

"Mother, do you need some thistledown?" asked Robin at her side, his tone implying that she obviously needed some padding for the quilt.

Fern glanced up at Balbo. They were both still hesitant to let their young son venture outside in this unknown land. A turtle dove started up a low cooing in the nearby forest.

"It's all right, you know. Let me go out. I won't be seen, or caught, or anything like that," said Robin, full of confidence.

The truth was, he had already been outside twice, slipping down a spider's silk rope made by Iris that he'd tied to the lattice window. There was a pile of dried leaves beneath the window, so even if he fell he would land safely. And it was around the back of the house, where Aunt Toyo never came.

"I wonder how Yahei is?" asked Iris. She was helping to stitch together the patchwork quilt cover. "Come to think of it, Robin, we really must ask Yuri to tie the marker ribbon on a tree so he can find us."

Robin gave up on going outside that day and retreated to the corner where he had his big book.

That evening Yuri arrived back home with a mixture of happiness and sadness on her face. As soon as she could, she went into the Little People's room carrying a small chipped bowl wrapped in a handkerchief, and poured its contents into the blue glass goblet behind the old sedge hat by the lattice window.

That night, for the first time in a long while, the Ashe Family could drink real goat's milk instead of the normal powdered milk. And when Yuri went as usual to collect the empty glass, she found next to it a small slip of paper. It was good-quality paper torn from a notebook, and on it were written some small, neat letters in pencil. It looked like Robin's writing.

A ribbon for our frend the pidgin pleeze. At top of tall tree pleeze. Will put here tomorrw. And thanx for nice milk!

R

It was the first time she had ever received a letter from the Little People and it set her heart racing. But what could they mean by a "ribbon for our frend the pidgin"?

She tore a page out of her schoolbook and wrote a reply.

> *A friend at school gave me the goat's milk. He's called Tsutomu. What is "a ribbon for our friend the pigeon"? If it's something I can do, I'll be happy to do it!*

She folded up the note and left it below the sedge hat.

Earlier Tsutomu had made her cry, and had given her the milk to make up for it. She had been thoroughly ashamed of herself for giving in to her own greediness and eating the treats that she had been saving for everyone at home, and was feeling quite miserable when Tsutomu had come hurtling down the slope and crashed right into her.

"Ship sunk! Ship sunk! The enemy ship *Pale Child of the East* has been sunk in the southern sea!" he'd yelled, mimicking the Imperial announcements broadcast on the radio. When he heard the chorus of his friends' reproachful voices, though, he quickly came back to the site of the "sinking" to find Yuri crouched on the path crying, her shoulders shaking. She was always so cheerful and smiling at school that the village children were quite taken aback at seeing her cry for the first time. By the time they reached the school, she had already dried her tears and just sat in the classroom in a daze, all alone and not talking to anyone.

After school, Tsutomu had been waiting for her on the path home and asked her if there was anything she wanted, and she'd said distractedly that she wanted some goat's milk. He told her to wait, and soon came back with a chipped red bowl half full of milk. He lived in a big farmhouse where they had a goat, he told her, and also that he hated goat's milk, but if she liked it he could bring her more so she should drink it up right away.

Yuri couldn't explain to her rough-and-tumble friend that he wasn't the only reason she had burst into tears. She spread out her handkerchief and carefully wrapped the bowl in it.

"Thank you!" she said, then set off up the path for home.

That night Yuri was so worn out from the grass-cutting and dinner was so late that she dozed off right afterwards.

Normally Aunt Toyo would have woken her up and made her lay out her bedding properly, but on the way home from the fields she had heard about how that rascal Tsutomu had made her cry, so for once she pretended not to notice when Granny Oto laid out the bedding for her. And she herself picked Yuri up and gently laid her down under the quilt that her mother Toko had made for her.

A NEW FRIEND

———

The next morning before school, Yuri peeked under the sedge hat. There, like a snake's cast-off skin, was a long, fluffy, rainbow-coloured ribbon neatly folded up on the windowsill. And, like yesterday, there was also a scrap of paper torn from a notebook.

Yuri hurriedly took her handkerchief out of the pocket of her baggy work trousers and folded the ribbon inside it. Then she picked up Robin's letter and set off up the hill for school. Once she reached the pass overlooking the lake, she squatted down by her usual rock and unfolded the little scrap of paper to read it.

Yahei the pidgin is from Tokyo. He is cuming to look for us. We tied a ribbon like this to his foot. Pleeze tie it to the top of a tree.

R

Yuri smiled to herself, imagining little Robin hugging a big pencil as he wrote this note.

I'm sorry, yesterday I ate the gift I was going to give you. But I found out that Tsutomu's got a goat. I'll make friends with him, and get lots of milk for you. And I'll get him to tie this ribbon on a tree for you too!

Yuri skipped lightly along the path to school.

Just after lunch, Robin heard footsteps in the back garden. He picked up Iris's rope and slipped out of their home on the shelf and down to the lattice window. Balbo and Fern were sleeping, wrapped up in their blanket and quilt, and so Iris came with him.

The pair peered out into the garden, which was bathed in the bright afternoon light of autumn. The footsteps belonged to Yuri, and a burly village boy dressed in long trousers. The two children were standing in the garden looking up at the larch forest and eagerly discussing something together.

"They're looking for a tree they can tie the ribbon to," Robin whispered to Iris.

The boy pointed to the tallest larch tree and said something. Yuri nodded, and handed him the sparkling ribbon.

The boy scooted up the tree in no time at all and tied the ribbon to a nail-bitingly high branch. Down below Yuri clapped her hands in delight.

"Yuri. Yuri!" came Granny Oto's voice.

Yuri tensed and called back, "Yes?"

The kitchen door opened, and Granny Oto came shuffling out into the back garden.

"Yuri, who is that over there?" her aunt asked.

"It's my friend Tsutomu, from school. He found a wood-pecker's nest in the tree. The woodpecker made a round hole in the trunk," Yuri answered with difficulty.

Granny Oto's white hair fluttered in the autumn breeze. "Stop playing such dangerous games," she said and went back into the house as steadily as any seeing person.

Up in the tree Tsutomu laughed, but Yuri stared at the kitchen door through which Granny Oto had disappeared as if deep in thought. Eventually Tsutomu came down from the tree and shook her out of her daze, and the pair disappeared from sight.

Robin and Iris stood by the window looking up at the ribbon in the tree. If it was seen by someone who didn't know any better, it might look a bit like a tangled spider's web, or a bit of rubbish. But to Robin and Iris the ribbon sparkled and shone just like a rainbow. If Yahei came this way, surely he would see the ribbon gleaming there and be able to find them. For the first time since coming to Nojiri, Iris looked reassured.

"Robin, let's go outside and find some dandelion down for Father's quilt!"

Treading softly, Iris went back up to the shelf to get her bag—the same shoulder bag that Robin had used to collect acorns outside the Moriyamas' house back in Tokyo.

The wall outside the lattice window had a rough coat of plaster, making it easy for Robin and Iris to get safely down the rope. The ground in the back garden was strewn with fallen leaves that rustled under their feet. They tied themselves together with rope, and wandered around looking for dandelion down, but it was September and it had all blown away in the breeze by now.

Treading softly, they made their way over to the inviting freshness of the larch forest. Some bird feathers floated lightly around them. Robin strained his eyes and stared into the shade of the forest. The rays of sunlight filtering down through the branches flickered on the ground, where something that looked like a small whirlwind was spinning round and round. The bird feathers were being whipped up by this wind.

"Bird feathers would be okay for the quilt, wouldn't they?" Robin whispered to his sister, and bounded off towards the whirlwind.

"Argh!" screamed Iris as the rope tying them together pulled taut and dragged her with him.

Coming to an abrupt halt, Robin found himself face to face with a strange little fellow. The two stared at each other for a while, then burst out laughing. In a voice that sounded like the rustling of dried leaves, the fellow said, "I do believe I've come across something strange 'ere."

Robin gulped.

"And there I was thinking you might be able to speak!" The barefoot, sunburnt little fellow cheerfully opened his eyes wide. "Are you after my feathers, young man?" he added, eyeing Robin sternly.

Iris went quietly up to him and spoke gently. "Hello! I'm Iris, and this is my little brother Robin."

The little fellow went a bit pink, and then said to Iris, "I don't have no name. Some might call me Amanejakki, though, I s'pose."

Iris and Robin looked at each other.

"You're wondering why I'm not surprised to see you. Aren't you now?" Amanejakki said in his hoarse voice. He seemed to be enjoying staying one hop, skip and jump ahead of them, and saying exactly what they had indeed been thinking.

"Yes, we were. It's really strange!" answered Iris seriously. "Why aren't you surprised? Have you seen people like us before?"

Amanejakki laughed teasingly, and began dancing around them like a little whirlwind. Robin was getting annoyed. He shook off Iris's hand and tried to catch him, but with a whistling kind of laugh the little whirlwind blew up dried leaves from the ground and disappeared off into the forest.

Robin and Iris exchanged another look, then called out after him "Hey! Hey, come back! Jakki!"

"Hey, come back! Jakki!" came back a faint voice from the edge of the forest, after which they heard nothing at all other than the calls of the coal tits and doves.

Iris and Robin stood stupefied there by the forest. At their feet, soft white feathers danced round and round and round.

Iris squatted down and began collecting up the feathers and putting them in her bag.

"Iris, don't do that. Don't you think they're a bit weird?"

"No, not at all. They're a gift to us from that Am-Ama... that Jakki. He knows we're looking for something to stuff a quilt with," said Iris, and carried on gathering them up.

"Wasn't he rude, spinning around us like that?" Robin was still in a huff.

Having picked up the last of the feathers, Iris laughed. "Robin, today's a really good day. Think about it. We finally put the ribbon marker up for Yahei, and we discovered that another Little Person other than us is living here, and on top of that we got some feathers for the quilt, didn't we?"

But the only point on which Robin agreed with his sister was that they should keep everything about today secret from their mother, and he remained in a sulky silence all the way back to their home on the shelf.

Meanwhile Yuri had been helping Tsutomu cut grass near his home. No men were left in his house, and Tsutomu, his elder brothers, one in middle school and the other in his last year of primary school, assisted his mother with the farm work. Yuri had come to help in exchange for some goat's milk.

There was a good view of the lake from Tsutomu's house.

"Yuri, have you ever been to that island there? It's called Benten Island," Tsutomu asked her.

Yuri told him how she had planned to get her brother Tetsu to take her there, but in the end they hadn't been able to go.

"It's great that your big brother is still alive, Yuri. My big brother died in battle in Bornco," said Tsutomu with a sigh as he swished the cutter through the grass. "My dad died before that in northern China, so my family's honoured for its war dead."

Shocked, Yuri didn't say anything.

"That's why we need to grow up quickly, join the army and

avenge our father and brother. Isn't your brother joining up, Yuri?"

Yuri thought as hard as she could, then told her friend that her brother Shin was going to the military preparatory school next year.

Tsutomu sighed and said enviously, "He's so lucky! I'm not clever enough to do that."

Tsutomu's trust in Yuri seemed to have grown after she told him about Shin, and he cut grass all the more quickly.

Yuri had been wondering whether or not she should tell this new friend of hers about the Little People, but now she decided to keep quiet about them. He would probably say she was being a traitor, the same as Shin had. There were certain things that other people could never understand, and she was glad she hadn't told Tsutomu that the ribbon she'd got him to tie on the tree was a marker to help a pigeon find his friends.

The two of them carried on cutting grass until their wooden frames were filled to overflowing, and then went back to Tsutomu's house.

The evening sun set surprisingly fast in the mountains and all of a sudden it was dark. When they reached the house, in the dim interior they could just make out Tsutomu's mother and elder sister kindling the fire in the cooking stove, while his brothers were already seated beside the sunken hearth. The harmonious sounds of family wafted out of the house to where they stood outside.

Their father may have died in northern China, and their elder brother in Borneo, but the remaining family members seemed to get on well. Standing outside waiting for Tsutomu,

Yuri gazed rapturously at the cosy scene inside, which seemed to her to shine like one single, happy lamp.

Tsutomu came round from the back of the house and called, "Yuri, where are you?" Then he caught sight of her lonely figure gazing into the house.

He pressed a warm bottle into her hands. "Yuri, come and cut grass for our goat again, all right? Shall I come some of the way back with you?"

Yuri said there was no need, but he followed her up the mountain path anyway. "When you walk along this path at night, you shouldn't look down. As long as you look up as you walk, you'll find your way okay."

She did as she was told, and saw that the tops of the dense, dark trees divided in two where the paths diverged. And two or three stars were twinkling brightly in the night sky, where the last of the daylight still lingered.

"Thank you, Tsutomu. I'll be okay from here!" Still looking up at the sky, Yuri ran quickly down the slope.

She could hear him singing a patriotic march as he went back down the path to his house.

That night, the Little People again found the blue glass goblet full to the brim of real goat's milk. It was such a treat to have some fresh milk when they had grown so used to that watery concoction of powdered milk. In the dim light, Fern began making some cheese to keep for emergencies. She caught sight of Iris slipping the bird feathers into the quilt cover, but she didn't scold her.

THE FIRST SNOW

———

By the time November came around, winter had settled over Nojiri.

Upon waking in the morning, Yuri could see her breath even inside the house and she found it really hard to get out of bed. It felt as though her back, still heavy with fatigue, was stuck to the warm mattress, and it took all her courage to tear it away and venture out into the piercing cold.

The leaves had fallen from the trees in the larch forest, and the peaks on the far side of the lake had already started turning white in October. Three mountains in a row, all different heights, were slightly different shades of white, the northernmost, Mount Myoko, being the whitest followed by Mounts Kurohime then Iizuna, sparkling below the blue sky.

A letter arrived regularly every week from Yuri's mother, Toko. She was always worried about Yuri's health. And it was through these letters that Yuri learnt about what was happening far away in Tokyo, such as the fact that her father had not yet returned home, her brother Shin got up at five o'clock every morning to go to kendo practice, and they had harvested five *kan* of sweet potatoes from their garden vegetable patch that autumn.

Yuri also wrote long letters in pencil to her mother. She told Mother everything, from how Aunt Toyo's rice crop had been safely harvested, to how the Little People were waiting for Yahei to arrive from Tokyo and the time she'd been mushroom-picking with her friend Tsutomu.

In reply to Yuri's question, Toko wrote that no pigeons came to the Moriyamas' garden in Tokyo any more. She seemed to have taken a shine to Tsutomu, for she often mentioned him in her letters. And so Yuri often wrote back to her about her rough-and-tumble classmate.

Meanwhile the Little People were each making their own preparations for winter. Balbo had started grinding acorn flour, as he had done in Tokyo. Fern got Iris to help her make two more quilts with the feathers that Amanejakki left for them every time he turned up in a whirlwind of dried leaves.

Robin was determined to catch him, but the little imp was always one step ahead. Iris couldn't bear the thought of him shivering in the wintry winds that blew through the mountains, and so she unpicked her own chilli-red sweater and used the wool to knit a cute waistcoat for him.

One day they heard his hoarse voice like the rustle of dried leaves calling them from the back garden: "Iriiiiis! Robiiiiiin!"

Iris picked up the finished waistcoat and slipped quietly down from the shelf. Robin followed after his sister. Now the leaves had fallen, the larch forest felt unusually spacious and light. Iris gazed into the thick of the trees and exchanged a glance with Robin. A strange squirrel-like creature was dancing round and round and round in there. It was about the same size as Amanejakki, and was on all fours. Iris stepped back in fright as the squirrel fur split open and the sunburnt face of that little imp popped out with a big grin on his face.

"Iriiis! I scared you!" Amanejakki laughed merrily.

"Yes, you did. You're a naughty boy, really!" Iris scolded him, hiding the red waistcoat behind her back.

Amanejakki opened his eyes wide. Then he said seriously, "You're hiding something from me, aren't you?"

"Yes. But you've got a magnificent fur coat, haven't you?" she said primly.

"It's for you. You'll ne'er get through the winter without one of these 'ere coats." He slipped nimbly out of the skin. Underneath it he was wearing another one. "Look, one fer Balbo, one fer Fern, and one fer Iris! And, last of all, one fer Robin!" he chanted in a sing-song voice, slipping out of yet more skins and throwing them onto the dry leaves on the ground. Underneath he was completely naked, and looked tiny.

"Robin, I betcha you won't wear something I made!" he added sarcastically, while trying to sneak a glimpse of what was behind Iris's back.

Iris flushed red. She had felt sorry for Amanejakki looking so scruffy and that's why she'd knitted the waistcoat for him, but who was she to be meddling in his life? He was an independent free spirit, a loner who didn't need anyone's sympathy. Amanejakki was staring at her with his piercing eyes. Then he let out a loud whoop and started dancing around.

"A waistcoat! A waistcoat fer me! She made me a waistcoat! I won't be naked any more!"

Iris threw the waistcoat at the little imp dancing around her. He caught it and, still prancing around, put his arms through it.

"A waistcoat fer me! A waistcoat fer me! She made me a waistcoat! I won't be naked any more!"

He looked like a fire spirit, prancing around in the forest in his bright-red waistcoat. Iris picked up a squirrel skin from the ground and pulled it over her shoulders. She wondered who had made these coats. They even had a warm hood on them.

"Ho ho!" Amanejakki said, and, whirling crazily around, he disappeared off into the forest.

Watching him go, Iris said to Robin, "I wonder why he's being so kind to us? If it wasn't for him, we would probably freeze to death."

Without a word, Robin picked up the remaining three skins off the ground. It was extremely annoying, but he had to admit she was right. *But what the heck* is *he? One of these days I'll work him out, you mark my words*, he thought to himself, glancing back at the forest as he followed after Iris, carrying the fluffy, heavy furs.

One day, Yuri was in the forest on the way to Hondo when she thought she could hear her brother Tetsu's voice. It was mid-November, about a week after the anniversary of Emperor Meiji's birthday.

She and Tsutomu had come to the chestnut groves on the way home from school. A fierce wind had been blowing as dawn broke, and Tsutomu said they'd be able to collect lots of fallen chestnuts. And there were indeed plenty of the brown burs on the ground beneath the low trees. Tsutomu adroitly split them open and took out the glossy nuts. However careful Yuri was, though, her hands kept getting pricked.

"Ow!" She gave up using her hands and instead gingerly stepped on them to split them open before carefully taking them out.

"Hey, your Korean shoes are strong, eh, Yuri?" Tsutomu laughed, looking at her feet.

Just then they heard a voice coming along the path—a young man's voice. Yuri pricked up her ears. That crisp Tokyo accent sounded just like Tetsu. Tsutomu also heard it and both of them strained to hear more. Then they heard a woman's voice. The two people seemed to be arguing about something as they walked.

Yuri and Tsutomu stuffed the chestnuts into the bags they had brought with them, and crept out of the grove. The people were walking along the path ahead of them.

"Tetsu?" Yuri could hardly believe her eyes and for a while just stared at their backs. Then with a loud cry she went bounding down the path. "Tetsu! *Tetsu!*"

The man wheeled round. It *was* Tetsu! Yuri flew into her brother's bear hug. *Why? Why did you come without telling me?!* Yuri wanted to reproach him but, held tight in her beloved brother's arms, she couldn't speak. She buried her head in his warm chest and wept big tears.

"Yuri, I'm sorry, I didn't mean to surprise you like this. Stop crying now. Everyone will laugh at you, you know!" Tetsu told her, jogging her in his arms.

Yuri suddenly remembered that he was with that woman Katsuko, and hurriedly extracted herself from his arms.

"Have you been out gathering chestnuts? When I arrived this morning you'd already left for school," he said, as if excusing himself.

Yuri couldn't bear the thought that her own brother had gone to see Katsuko before her. Katsuko was standing on the side of the path with a serious look on her face, impatiently waiting to continue the conversation.

Yuri picked up her bag of chestnuts and looked around for Tsutomu. He was crouching amidst the ears of pampas grass a little up ahead, watching them with his black eyes. She went and joined him and the pair walked on ahead of Tetsu, kicking the flat pebbles on the path.

That evening they enjoyed a cheerful dinner, with Aunt Toyo's delicious chestnut rice which she made to go with the canned salmon that Tetsu had brought from Tokyo. Tetsu had also brought a can of milk for Balbo and his family, which he gave to Yuri out of sight of the two women.

Tetsu had become so thin since his last visit in August that Aunt Toyo barely recognized him, and she urged him to eat more.

"No thanks, I don't want to get fat," muttered Tetsu jokingly.

Aunt Toyo retorted incredulously, "You don't want to get fat at your age? Just when everyone's building up their strength for the sake of our country!"

Tetsu laughed and said, "Our country? It's good to be able to believe in it... Shin's getting up at five every morning to go to kendo practice, you know."

Aunt Toyo looked at Tetsu suspiciously. "You're like Tatsuo, aren't you? If you're not careful, you'll end up like him—" Granny Oto tugged at her sleeve and she clamped her mouth shut.

Watching the shadows playing over Tetsu's thin face in the light from the hearth, Yuri felt scared. As they'd made their way home through the sea of white tufts of pampas grass that afternoon, Yuri hadn't completely understood what Katsuko and Tetsu had been talking about, but it was something terrible that she'd never heard about in school or in her aunt's house.

"All the men are laying down their lives for the sake of our country without complaining, aren't they? So we women want to do something for the sake of our country too, you know."

"While you unwittingly sacrifice yourselves like that, there are people profiting from this war. My father was taken away from us just for always saying how stupid this war is—because in our country we aren't allowed to criticize people in authority."

Yuri didn't hear Katsuko's reply, but after that the two of them had fallen into a chilly silence as they walked along the mountain path through the swaying pampas grass.

Seeing Tetsu's face looking just like it had that afternoon, Yuri felt afraid. She stood by the hearth adding kindling to the fire, making bright flames shoot up.

"Yuri, you've really become a Nojiri kid, haven't you? Tending the fire's second nature to you now," said Tetsu, changing the subject.

Just then the grandfather clock in the other room sleepily chimed eight.

"Well then, Yuri, time for bed. I expect you're looking forward to having Tetsu sleep with you again after so long," said Granny Oto.

Yuri stood up and went to lay out the bedding for her and Tetsu in the other room.

The next afternoon Tetsu took Yuri to Benten, the island she saw every day. He had borrowed a boat from one of Aunt Toyo's acquaintances on the lakeside, and rowed smoothly across the water. The breeze on the lake was icy, and Yuri felt her cheeks would freeze.

Tetsu told Yuri how beautiful the autumn colours were at Kokedera, the famous moss temple in Kyoto. Here on Benten, cedar trees grew thickly around them, and moss-covered steps led all the way up to the top of the mountain. When they reached the small shrine on the summit, Yuri put her hands together and prayed to the goddess Benten.

"Please let me go back to Tokyo soon. And please let Daddy come home soon. And please make Tetsu healthy again."

Tetsu took a picture of her standing under the trees by the shrine. And then she adjusted the focus and took a picture of him in return. Seeing him through the viewfinder, she thought he looked terribly lonely, and wondered if perhaps Katsuko was supposed to have come with them today.

They crossed back over the clear waters of the lake to the landing place right below Yuri's school. People were casting them disapproving glances. A little evacuee and her camera-toting brother going on a boat trip at a time like this must have seemed awfully frivolous to them.

The evening Tetsu was to leave, the first snow of winter fell in Nojiri. Yuri went to see him off, but he left her at the rock on the pass and went on alone. Aunt Toyo and Granny Oto had filled his big rucksack with treats like azuki beans, apples and buckwheat flour for him to take back to Tokyo, and the straps dug into his thin shoulders under the weight.

"Goodbye!"

"Goodbyeee!" Tetsu called out at the top of his lungs, then disappeared into the dark forest. The trees stood out starkly against the snow, giving the scene the effect of an ink painting.

The fluffy snowflakes landed on Yuri's hood and eyelashes and melted as she made her way back down the mountain path alone. The snow was like a living creature, hissing as it fell, and erased the footprints she and Tetsu had left earlier.

YAHEI AND AMANEJAKKI

The frequent snowfalls soon covered Yuri's house and surroundings in a mantle of white, and at about the same time everyone around her too began behaving coldly towards her.

After Tetsu's second visit, at school and the neighbouring houses around the mountainside people's attitude towards her started changing, although she didn't notice anything amiss to begin with.

One day she stopped by Tsutomu's house on the way home. Tsutomu was always so healthy, but she hadn't seen him at school for two or three days, and so she went to find out how he was. Wearing the warm snow boots Granny Oto had woven out of straw for her, she climbed up the path leading to his house. In the fresh snow at the side of the trail were some cute little tracks left by birds. It looked as if the birds had enjoyed a stroll in the snow, and she was reminded of the footprints left by Iris and Robin.

Standing sedately in the shade of the trees blanketed by snow, Tsutomu's farmhouse looked like a scene on a chocolate box. Yuri peered through the open kitchen door to its dark interior, and called, "Hello! Tsutomu, are you there?"

Tsutomu's mother rose from her place by the bright fire in the hearth.

"Hello, is Tsutomu sick?" Yuri asked her.

Tsutomu's mother looked Yuri up and down suspiciously. She seemed like a completely different person to the kindly woman who had given Yuri some freshly picked persimmons the last time she'd been over.

"I'm Tsutomu's classmate. He hasn't been at school, so..." Yuri added hurriedly, thinking maybe she had forgotten who she was.

"Tsutomu's got a cold and is in bed with a fever all right," the mother said irritably, looking at Yuri's worried face. "You're that Moriyama girl who evacuated from Tokyo, aren't you? So where's your father, then?"

Yuri looked at her in surprise. This was the first time she'd ever been asked about her father since coming to Nojiri.

"My father's in Tokyo."

"Is he now. Well, I don't suppose you'll tell me *where* in Tokyo he is?" She gave the kitchen door a rough shake with her big hands, as if warning a repulsive child to go away and stay away.

Yuri chewed at her thumbnail so hard it hurt and, trying to ignore her mocking tone, did her best to keep her pale face composed.

"Please tell Tsutomu I hope he gets better soon."

She had done her best to sound as placatory as possible, but Tsutomu's mother slammed the door shut in her face and said from the other side, "Tsutomu won't be playing with you any more. We're a respectable family with honourable war dead here. I won't let any son of mine play with the child of a traitor."

Yuri straightened her shoulders and set off back along the snowy path. *If you hold your head up as you walk, you'll find the sky is lighter along the path,* Tsutomu had once told her, and that's what she did now. Above the bare branches of the trees, the sky was bright blue.

Did Tsutomu hear what Tetsu and Katsuko were talking about? I was scared listening to them, but could he really have understood them? Her head burned as she tried hard to think. *Mummy told me that Daddy was taken to that place by mistake. Shin said he was taken there because he was bad, but I believe Mummy. There's no way Daddy can be a traitor, not with the way he smiled at me so gently in that place. But if he is a traitor, that means Tetsu is also, and maybe me too.*

The mountain path that day had appeared to be deserted, and Yuri couldn't have known that some villagers had been working nearby and overheard every word of Tetsu and Katsuko's conversation. They had been scandalized by his being out enjoying a walk together with a girl at such a critical time, and the fact that on top of that he was saying bad things about the army and the war just inflamed their antipathy all the more. Rumours about him had spread like wildfire throughout the area, and even those who had known about Tatsuo Moriyama but had kept quiet about him until now nodded knowingly and said, "Like father, like son" and began falling over each other to tell everyone everything they knew about the Moriyama family.

And Tsutomu's mother, too, had been horrified to hear that the polite little evacuee's father was a traitor and in prison.

Yuri ran down the rest of the path as if trying to shake off something unpleasant, and arrived back at Aunt Toyo's house. When she took off her red gloves, she noticed a blood blister in the shape of a tooth under the nail of her right thumb, and the thumb throbbed painfully. But she didn't say anything. As always, she made up some powdered milk for Balbo and his family, and the blue glass goblet soothed her aching heart. *One day you'll be able to live together with your father and the rest of your family again*, it seemed to be telling her.

What will I do if Tsutomu won't play with me any more? He's been so nice! If he starts being nasty to me, everyone at school will start bullying me, she thought as she placed the milk for the Little People by the window then went back to the kitchen. But in her heart of hearts she could hear a little voice whisper, *It'll be all right, Yuri. Don't let it get you down!* She thought it sounded like her mother Toko's voice. Or it might have been Fern.

"That's right. I'll never give in!" she said to herself and, before being told by Aunt Toyo, went out to the shed to get some kindling to light the fire in the hearth.

Tsutomu was lying in another room when he thought he heard Yuri call out to him.

"Mama, did someone come over just now?" he asked in a rasping voice from under a pile of bedding.

"No, nobody. I just closed the kitchen door because it's getting cold," she answered sullenly from the kitchen.

Unconvinced, Tsutomu persisted, "But I heard you saying I couldn't play with someone... who can't I play with?"

"That evacuee girl you're always hanging around with," she spat back at him. "Your big brother says her father is a traitor and in prison, you know. I'm not having you play with someone like that."

Tsutomu didn't answer. An image of Yuri's white face appeared in his still-feverish mind. He just couldn't reconcile that terrible word "prison" with the sight of her weeping in the sunset. He'd heard his brother saying bad things about Yuri's big brother too, but he hadn't seemed at all like a traitor when he'd met him on the mountain path, although he had looked terribly thin and serious.

Then something occurred to him. *She said her other brother is at military prep school, didn't she? So he can't be a traitor. And she isn't either*, he muttered to himself. *I will play with her!*

This made him feel much better, and he fell fast asleep.

That night, in the Little People's house, Balbo and Fern spread Yuri's blanket from the basket on the floor like a carpet, and wrapped themselves up in all the bedding they had, but even so they lay awake shivering. Iris and Robin were wearing the squirrel skins and sleeping peacefully with just their usual bedding to cover them.

"The children have been going outside again, haven't they?"

Fern whispered to Balbo. "No, I'm not going to stop them. Seeing them coming home with glowing cheeks, I can well imagine how much fun they're having out there."

As Balbo didn't answer, she continued, "On the other hand, did you see Yuri's face this evening? I felt so terribly sorry for her that I couldn't help telling her, *Don't let it get you down!* That child is holding back on something. Maybe something terrible is starting again?"

Balbo cleared his throat and said, "Stop talking and go to sleep. It's snowing again. That's what it sounds like, anyway."

In the dark they could hear the rustle of freezing snow landing on the thatched roof. The old wooden ceiling creaked as it, too, froze.

"I wonder how things are in Tokyo now? Perhaps we shouldn't have run away here to such a cold place," Fern spoke up again. But Balbo didn't answer, and so she gave up and buried her face beneath her feather quilt.

Unknown to either Fern or Balbo, the skies over Tokyo at that moment were full of B-29s dropping an endless stream of incendiary bombs and burning down houses.

Japan was losing the war it had started, but the only people who knew this were those few who had dragged the country into the war in the first place. Nobody else had any idea of the situation, and carried on sleeping as peacefully as Iris and Robin. Either that or they were like Fern and Balbo, shivering under the bedclothes unable to sleep for the cold.

Over them all, the snow kept steadily falling with a soft swishing sound.

*   *   *

The next morning the weather was glorious. Iris and Robin put on their shoes and the squirrel-fur coats Amanejakki had given them, and prepared to go outside. Careful not to wake their sleeping parents, they started to quietly lower themselves down on the rope.

Just then there was a tremendous flapping of wings outside. *Coo-coo coo-coo coo-coo!* came a familiar voice.

"It's Yahei!"

"Yahei's found us!"

They hurried down from the shelf and pushed open the lattice window, which creaked against the weight of the snow piled against it, and raced into the dazzling world outside. A lone pigeon was flying in low circles above the trees.

The rainbow-coloured ribbon that Tsutomu had tied to a larch branch last autumn was hidden under snow. Would Yahei see them? Iris waved the spider's silk rope as hard as she could, hoping to catch Yahei's eye. Robin began running over the snow towards the tree, thinking he could climb it and brush the snow off the ribbon. Just then a little whirlwind appeared, sending up a shower of powdery snow as it spun round and round.

Up above, Yahei noticed a pretty white whirlwind on the ground. Something was kicking up a storm in the snow in the back garden of the house below him. He landed on the roof of the house to take a better look. In the middle of the whirlwind was some kind of fiery red creature. Then he heard a crystalline voice like a silver thread snapping in his ear.

"Ya-he-iiii! It's us, Iris and Robin! We're here!"

Coo-coo! he replied, and flew down to the ground. The white whirlwind brushed passed his feet, and an unfamiliar laugh rang out. Then, just beyond the white haze of snow, he saw his beloved Iris waving something shiny around.

"Iris!" he called. He'd found them at last! Careful not to startle his little friends, he hopped slowly over to them. "Iris, I'm glad to see you looking so well."

"Yahei, I'm so happy to see you!" Iris smiled up at him, her face pink like a hyacinth blooming on the snow.

Robin was stuck in a snowdrift under the trees, kicking his legs as hard as he could to free himself, desperate to join Yahei and his sister, but the harder he kicked the deeper he sank into the snow and was unable to move.

"Ha ha ha ha!" the white whirlwind laughed in his ear. "Right now you're hoping I'll help you, aren't you?"

Amanejakki pulled him out of the snow and, still spinning, took him over to Yahei and Iris. Yahei looked at Amanejakki in surprise. Then he noticed Robin and said nostalgically, "Robin, it's you! We meet again at last. Won't you tell your friend to keep still a moment? He's making me dizzy."

Hearing this, Amanejakki began spinning for all he was worth, like a mole trying to rid its entire body of fleas. It was as if ten of him had appeared in the garden.

But Iris knew how to deal with him. "Faster faster faster!" she said in her best big-sisterly voice. "Now come over here next to me!"

Amanejakki suddenly quietened down, then disappeared into the forest at the end of the garden, his red waistcoat blazing.

"What on earth was *that*?" asked Yahei, astounded.

So Iris told Yahei about their strange new friend. "That little imp likes guessing what you're going to say before you say it. And if you want him to do something, you have to tell him to do the opposite. He's really funny! And he's kind, too. If it wasn't for him, you'd never have seen us just now, would you?"

Then she told him about the rainbow-coloured ribbon tied to the branch on the tree.

"Really? I was thinking you'd already forgotten me. I came to Nojiri at the end of August, and have been looking for you since then, you know. I'm really glad we've finally met up again. We're living in a town just the other side of the lake. It's a bit warmer there than it is here."

"We? Are your parents with you?" asked Robin.

"No, they're in Nagano," Yahei said a bit shyly. "While I was looking for you, I met a pretty white pigeon, and I've been living with her."

He turned to Iris. "She's very keen to meet both of you, too. She really likes this rainbow ribbon, and wants one of her own, so I told her that it was a sign for my dear friends Iris and Robin and I couldn't give it to her. But she told me that when I found you, I should ask you for another one for her."

Iris laughed in delight, and promised Yahei she would give him a ribbon to take to her.

"Yahei, please let me fly with you again!" Robin couldn't contain himself any longer. "I've been longing to get on your back and fly through the sky again!"

Yahei happily held out his grey wing for him.

"Oh, we've finally found you. And what's more, there's not just one, but two of you now! We'll never part from you ever again!" said Iris, with a sigh of relief, waving the sparkling rope at Robin as he rode on Yahei's back.

THE LAST OF THE MILK

———

Winter in Nojiri froze everything, from the well water to the jars of pickles and the Little People's milk. As New Year passed and February came, it grew even more severe.

Balbo and Fern were overwhelmed by hunger and the cold, and stayed in bed all day long. Now and then Yuri would heat a stone in the hearth and bring it wrapped in a cloth to the Little People's home. This was their only form of heating.

Just as Fern had feared, Yuri seemed to be having a terrible time at school. But she didn't utter a word of complaint to Aunt Toyo or Granny Oto. At first, Tsutomu had played with her at school, but then he'd been severely scolded by his mother and stopped talking to her. Even if he bumped into her on the way to school he pretended he hadn't seen her. And so Yuri found herself shunned by the group and was left with no one to play with. She started coming straight home from school and sat by the hearth learning how to make straw sandals with Granny Oto. This was the homework school had set for her. She also learnt how to twist straw into a rope to help meet the local supply quotas set by the army.

In February, the air raids on Tokyo and Osaka grew even fiercer, and news of them reached even here in the mountains of Nojiri. Yahei told Iris that big groups of evacuee children had arrived in the town where he was living, and whenever the radio announced that a large number of enemy planes were headed for Tokyo, many of them burst into tears worrying about their parents.

Sometimes Yahei would bring his wife, a white pigeon called Tama, to visit Robin and Iris. They were looking forward to moving to the nearby forest once the winter was over. One day in March, Yahei saw some bird's-eye primroses blooming through the snow and hurried over to Robin and Iris with one of the flowers to bring them the good news.

"It's spring! Spring is just round the corner!"

But the house in the mountains was shrouded in deathly silence. Yahei poked the flower into a gap in the lattice window, then flew up into the larch tree as usual.

"Coo coo!" he called.

After a while, Robin came out alone.

"What's the matter, Robin? You don't look very well. But spring has already arrived in town, you know. Did you see the flower I brought you?" Yahei asked enthusiastically.

Robin shook his head.

Yahei looked at him in surprise. "What's up? Are you sick?"

Robin shook his head again. Then he said, as if forcing it out, "The house in Tokyo burned down. Our little book room burned too. Poor Yuri's fallen ill."

Yahei ducked his head and spread his wings. "Is it serious?"

Robin shook his head as if to say he didn't know. "Iris was crying with her too. Yuri's got a really high fever. Sometimes she cries out in her dreams."

Yahei shook his head sorrowfully. "Oh dear, so that house burned down too. That old house by the big zelkova tree, right? Well, I'm going home now. Please give that flower to Yuri. Tell her that spring will be here soon, okay?"

Robin watched his big friend fly off into the sky over the forest until he disappeared, and then dragged himself back to the house.

Robin picked up the flower that had fallen down outside the window and took it to Yuri's bedside. Yuri was motionless, sleeping.

Granny Oto had stayed at her side the whole night, but now she went through to the hearth in the kitchen and the only sound to be heard in the room was the *tick tock* of the grandfather clock.

By Yuri's pillow was the letter from Toko giving a brief account of the air raid on 10th March.

...On 10th March our house burned down. I am now reflecting on how glad I am that I sent you to Nojiri, Yuri. There have been many times when I wondered if

it was a mistake to let you go all on your own when you're so young. But Yuri, had you and the others been here, I would have had to worry about all of you too during that terrible night.

Your brother Shin was a huge help, you know. He was far calmer than I was. When the incendiary bombs started raining down on us he took all our essentials out of the house and put them in the shelter while I just watched all our trees in the garden go up in flames, like Christmas tree lights coming on. Our last remaining patch of lawn and the plot where I was growing sweet potatoes soon went up too, surrounding us in flames. Shin pulled me by the hand and ran towards a place that didn't seem to be on fire. In the smoke we passed by Mrs Ikeda from next door and said goodbye as we each went our different ways. We never spoke very much, but it was like talking to a dear old friend. I haven't seen her since.

The next morning, when I went back to our house, it wasn't there. All that was left of our beloved little book room was a pile of book-shaped ashes, still smoking. It all burned down—everything! But Yuri, you and the Little People are safe and sound, and Shin, Tetsu and Daddy are all alive. That gives me the strength to pick myself up and look for somewhere new to live.

Now Shin and I are living at the address on the envelope. From here I don't have so far to go to see Daddy.

Well, take care of yourself Yuri. Shin sends his love too.

When the letter had arrived the day before, Yuri had had to read it out aloud to Aunt Toyo and Granny Oto. When she finished, Aunt Toyo had commented how spineless Toko was. How come she had just run away instead of putting out the incendiary bombs as they fell? Yuri had kept her eyes downturned, chewing on her finger. Then she went out to the shed to get firewood, and didn't come back for a long time.

Late that night, she had come down with a fever and a fit of wheezing like her long-forgotten asthma that left her hardly able to breathe. Granny Oto stayed by her side, rubbing her back. Yuri tried to escape her, and cried out in her dreams, gasping for breath.

All night long red flames burned in Yuri's eyes. Big zelkova trees burned like so many Christmas trees. Beneath them her house became a ball of fire and sent sparks up into the sky. Inside she could hear Balbo and Fern calling *Help! Help us!* Would Robin and Iris burn to death too? No, no! They mustn't! Yuri writhed and shouted, *Don't die!* She could hear Robin's and Iris's voices coming from the midst of the sparks flying up into the sky, *Goodbye, Yuri, goodbye!*

Yuri smelt the fresh scent of flowers, and opened her eyes. A pure white sweet-smelling flower lay beside her pillow. Next to it, little Robin was looking up at her anxiously.

Oh, thank goodness! Robin and the others didn't die after all. Robin's here with me! She tried to reach out for the flower, but she felt as though she'd been beaten black and blue and lacked the strength even to move her hand.

Thank you! she told Robin with her eyes. Robin went nervously up to her and placed the flower on the edge of her bedding. Then he looked up at her with his sparkling brown eyes, as if to say *Get better soon!* and left her alone.

Around noon, Granny Oto came shuffling into the room, and held her hand on Yuri's forehead. It felt pleasantly cool.

"What can I get for you?" she asked. "If you tell me what you want to eat, I'll make it for you. Tell me what you want."

Yuri couldn't answer. Right now she wanted something cold and sweet. What was it her mother Toko always brought her when she was sick? She squeezed her eyes shut and tried to remember. Ice cream? Stewed apples? That was it! Right now, what she wanted was thinly sliced apples stewed in sugar and chilled.

When she didn't answer, Granny Oto told her, "If you don't eat anything, you won't get better quickly. Last night you kept saying you wanted milk. Wasn't there a can of milk in your emergency bag?"

Yuri's heart started pounding. Had she let on about the milk while she was feverish? Or maybe blind old Granny Oto had already cottoned on to the Little People some time ago? Various possibilities whirled around her tired head.

If I tell Granny Oto that I want some milk, maybe she'll open that can of condensed milk and make some up for me. If I don't drink all of it, the Little People will be able to finish it. But is it okay to do that? I'm supposed to put the milk in the blue glass goblet for them myself, but if I have to stay in bed for a few days, sooner or later I'll have to ask Granny Oto to make some for me… in which case it might as well be now, I suppose.

With her heart in her mouth, Yuri asked, "Could you make me a little milk?"

Granny Oto looked relieved, and went off to the kitchen. Yuri worried how she would manage to open the can. And how come she knew about the milk? But she soon returned carrying a tray, upon which she'd placed a coffee bowl that Yuri had never seen before filled with hot milk, and sat by Yuri's pillow to help her drink it. But Yuri had wanted cold milk.

"Later, Granny Oto. I'll drink it later," she said.

Granny Oto put the bowl down on the tray, and held her hand to Yuri's forehead again. Yuri closed her eyes. After a while, Granny Oto quietly rose and shuffled out of the room.

Yuri opened her eyes. Steam was still rising from the milk.

"Robin! Iris! Come here, please! Come and take this milk!" she whispered, her mouth dry. "Bring the blue glass goblet and take some of it, quick!"

Fern and the others heard Yuri calling. Balbo and Fern looked at each other. Robin and Iris started to fix the rope to go and get the milk right away.

"Is it okay to do this?" muttered Fern timorously.

But what else could they do? Balbo told the children, "Okay go, and take the blue glass goblet. But if you hear footsteps don't make a sound. If that old woman doesn't hear anything, she won't notice you're there."

Robin and Iris went down the rope, and took the glass from beneath the old sedge hat. Then, as quietly as they could, they climbed onto the tray and scooped up some milk from the bowl. Iris's heart pounded at the faint sound of the glass scraping the edge of the bowl. Robin licked the milk from the rim of the glass. Yuri closed her eyes.

The two Little People crept back up to the shelf carrying the glass. It wasn't easy but, thanks to Yuri, today the family could drink their fill of warm, sweet milk.

A while later, Yuri opened her eyes. About half the milk was gone. She reached out a shaky hand, picked up the bowl and took a sip of the now cold milk. It tasted just like the ice cream she'd dreamt of earlier. Cradling the bowl in both hands, she drank up the rest of it.

When Granny Oto came padding back in a little later, Yuri was fast asleep. Fumbling around with her hands, Granny Oto checked that the bowl was empty then, after straightening the bedclothes, took the bowl back to the kitchen.

This unusual arrangement between Yuri and the Little People family was to continue for some time. Yuri's fever didn't go away for several days, and she couldn't keep anything but milk down. Aunt Toyo was so worried about her that she went some distance in the snow to get hold of some eggs and apples, but Yuri couldn't face the slimy raw eggs. She happily ate the apple that Aunt Toyo mashed for her, but other than that she took nothing other than milk for ten days.

Luckily Robin and Iris were able to help themselves to some milk from the bowl by Yuri's pillow without ever being suspected by the Big People.

"Balbo, how long can we go on like this?" Fern asked anxiously from time to time. She was old-fashioned and couldn't bear the thought of taking food from the same cup as a human, persisting in the old belief that they should live off the milk brought to them in the blue glass goblet.

Robin and Iris laughed at their mother for this superstition, but soon Fern's worry took a different tack. "Iris, Robin! Are you sure you didn't spill any of the milk when you were bringing it back?" she asked one day, seeing that the blue glass goblet was only about two-thirds full.

"That's all there was today," Iris replied quietly.

"Yuri drank it before us. She usually waits for us to take some first," Robin grumbled, remembering how difficult it had been to scoop the milk into the glass from the bottom of the bowl.

Fern didn't say anything.

The next day, Robin and Iris brought the blue glass goblet back only just over half full. Fern sighed.

"It can't be helped. Yuri is getting better. When you recover from an illness, you get terribly hungry," said Balbo to smooth things over.

The next day the blue glass was barely half full. Fern took out some of her emergency cheese to make up the meagre meal.

The following day, the Little People watched from the shelf as Yuri tried to resist reaching out for the bowl. First she took just a sip of milk, then snuggled back down into bed. And then, just as Iris and Robin were on their way down from the shelf, she couldn't stand it any longer and reached out a hand from under the quilt and gulped down some milk before quickly burying herself back under the covers.

That day, Iris and Robin took home the blue glass just a third full of milk, barely any at all.

"Yuri doesn't seem to be thinking about us any more," complained Robin. "She must know there's hardly any left for us!"

Neither Fern nor Balbo said anything. Iris looked as though she was about to cry, and retreated into a corner of the room.

The next day, when Yuri asked Granny Oto to make up some milk she replied uncomfortably, "Yuri, there's no more milk after today. I've somehow made it last this long by mixing it with that powdered milk you had. But it's gone now, so be a good girl and have some rice broth or porridge instead."

Yuri sat up with a start. "Really? No more milk?"

Granny Oto was taken aback by Yuri's furious reaction and opened her unseeing eyes wide. "Yes really. It's all gone. Think about it, Yuri, you've been sick for over a fortnight now and all you've had during that time is milk."

Yuri burst into tears. Granny Oto frowned. She had spoilt her too much while she was sick and she was behaving just like a baby—but once she understood there really was no milk, she would have no choice but to eat something else. She went back out to the kitchen to heat up the last of the milk for her.

Yuri was still crying in bed, chewing her thumbnail.

I'm sorry! Balbo, Fern, Iris, Robin... I knew I shouldn't but in the end I drank all your milk. I knew there wasn't much left, but I kept thinking, just a little more, it'll be okay, just a little more. And now I've drunk it all up! What will become of you? I can't go and ask Tsutomu for some any more. And I can't go to Hondo while I'm sick in bed. There's still too much snow outside. Oh, what can I do? Iris, Robin... I hope you don't die!

Yuri heard Granny Oto come shuffling back into the room. As usual, she put down the tray and went away again. Torn between wanting to drink the milk and knowing Iris and the others would die if she did, Yuri huddled down under the covers and bit her thumbnail hard.

Hurry! Hurry! Robin, come and take the milk quickly. It's the last of the milk, so at least this time take the blue glass goblet full to the brim. Eventually she couldn't stand it any longer and peeped out from under the covers to see that half the milk had gone from the bowl. Relieved, she drank the rest of the bowl down.

If I ask Aunt Toyo, I'm sure she'll be able to get hold of some goat's milk for me.

The next day, bowing to Yuri's desperate entreaties, Aunt Toyo packed up some rice to exchange for milk and went out in the snow. But in that cold March weather, she couldn't get hold of even a single drop of milk to give to a sick child.

"Yuri, you'll have to make do with rice broth. Stop being so selfish!"

However much Granny Oto tried to persuade her, though, Yuri said nothing.

That evening Yuri was startled by the sound of a pigeon flapping its wings in the garden. And later that night she went down with a fever again, and had nightmares of a terrible fire. From inside the red flames that had engulfed the little book room, she could hear Balbo and Fern calling, *Help! Help us! Yuri, help!*

Yuri tossed and turned in her sleep. *No! No no no! You can't die! Iris, Robin, I don't want you to burn to death!*

THE LITTLE PEOPLE GO AWAY

———

The day after Yuri's condition worsened, an unfamiliar young woman in a headscarf turned up at Aunt Toyo's house covered in snow. She had heard that the Moriyama evacuee girl was sick and so had come to see her, she told them.

"Tetsu asked me some time ago to keep an eye on her, and to take her some goat's milk to drink from time to time. It's not the right season for milking, but I brought what little I could."

Aunt Toyo stared suspiciously at the young woman. Even she could guess that this was one of those "Salt of the Earth" women who had evacuated from Tokyo to Hondo. Nevertheless, she was grateful for the milk and showed the young woman into Yuri's room.

Katsuko gazed at Yuri sleeping quietly. She felt terribly moved by the sight of her flat body, so slight it was as if there was nothing there under the quilt, and gently ran her fingers through her tangled hair on the dirty pillow. At her touch, Yuri opened her eyes and stared at her in surprise.

"Yuri, don't worry, it's me. Drink lots of goat's milk and get better soon, okay?" Katsuko said, placing a bottle by her pillow.

Great tears welled up in Yuri's eyes, and became an unstoppable flow down her cheeks as she mumbled something.

"Oh? What was late? Me coming here?"

Yuri shook her head and said something else, but all Katsuko could catch was, "It's too late! Too late!"

Yuri was staring up at the ceiling. Katsuko began to feel bad. It wasn't right for such a small girl as Yuri to be so alone, and so desperate. She stroked her head and said soothingly, like a doctor, "Tell me what's on your mind. If it's something I can help with, I will. Tell me everything that's bothering you, Yuri."

Yuri didn't say anything for a long time. Then all of a sudden she began weeping with great convulsive sobs.

"They've gone! They've gone! They've gone and left me!" she wailed.

"Who have? Your mother? Tetsu?" asked Katsuko frantically, on the verge of tears herself.

Yuri shook her head. Then, plucking up courage, she said, "Katsuko, will you look under that sedge hat and see if there is a blue glass there?"

Katsuko did as she was told and looked under the hat. There, just as Yuri had said, was a beautiful small sky-blue glass. She handed it to Yuri.

Yuri took it in both hands, and stroked it lovingly. Then she looked Katsuko straight in the eye and said, "Will you look on top of that shelf near the ceiling and tell me what you see? Behind those books up there."

Again, Katsuko did as she was told and stepped on the conveniently placed wooden chest so that she could peer onto the smoke-stained shelf.

"There's nothing here. Except this book, that is." Katsuko took the yellow book and sat down with it beside Yuri's pillow. It was Robin's beloved book with the tiger in it that he had left behind.

"You didn't see anything other than that? Nothing at all?"

Katsuko shook her head in silence.

Yuri had stopped crying and was staring unseeingly at Robin's book. It was getting dark outside. Worried that she might have outstayed her welcome on her first visit to the house, Katsuko asked, "May I come and see you again?"

Yuri gave a slight nod.

"In that case, I'll bring some more goat's milk with me next time. And when you start going back to school in spring, come over to visit me sometimes too, won't you?"

Yuri nodded again.

"Is there anything you want me to do?"

Yuri thought for a moment. Then she said clearly, "Put some of the goat's milk in this glass and put it back in the same place."

Katsuko wondered uneasily whether Yuri was delirious with fever, but she did as she was told.

"Thank you!" Yuri said. For the first time something approaching a smile played around the corners of her mouth.

Katsuko gently patted the bedding in a sisterly fashion, and then left.

Aunt Toyo and Granny Oto told her that they sincerely hoped she would come again as they saw her off.

Not long before, Katsuko had received notice from Tetsu Moriyama that he had enrolled at Kyoto University on 25th March and was now joining the air force, so it wouldn't be long before he was sent off to war.

She had gone to see his little sister wanting to at least inform her that the house in Tokyo had burned down on 10th March, and that Tetsu had now joined the military he hated so much, but now her heart felt heavier than ever. Whatever that little girl had lost when she came here, something must have happened that was even worse than just being ripped from her family. What on earth could have caused such desperation in the little girl?

As Katsuko climbed up the mountain path, she thought to herself that she would do whatever it took to see even just the trace of a smile on little Yuri's thin face. The child really needed a friend. If they started up the children's group again in the spring, she would have to get Yuri involved in it.

Katsuko trudged home alone over the cold snow as the clouds above were lit up by a magnificent sunset.

AT AMANEJAKKI'S

Late April came round and at last the long winter was over. The snow on the distant peaks disappeared in exactly the reverse order of its arrival, first from Mount Iizuna, lingering on with the patchy snow near the summit of Mount Kurohime, and Mount Myoko still with its sparkling silver winter cover. The mountain birds began singing in the light blue of the dawn, and continued singing in the forests around the lake after the sun had set, expressing their joy at the arrival of spring.

Robin wandered through the flowers with his bag slung over his shoulder. The ground cover of violets, dandelions and fawn lilies was complemented by bushes of vermilion quince blossoms, and higher up on the slopes the cherry, magnolia, plum and apricot trees briefly bloomed to the accompanying buzz of bee wings.

Spring in the mountains comes from below! That was what Amanejakki had said in an unusually candid moment just a fortnight before—and gazing at the skirts of the nearby mountains, he could see that it was true. Spring in the mountains dyed the woods pale pink from the bottom up, and now even the higher slopes were enveloped in the warm pink clouds of blossom, while the lower woods were carpeted with spring flowers.

Robin stepped lightly among them, collecting sweet nectar from the flowers with violet petals. His first stroll of spring was more fun than he could ever have imagined during the long years he'd spent confined to the house in Tokyo. It had been just about this time last year that he had witnessed spring for the first time in his life. He had been astonished by its beauty then, but the wonder of spring in Nojiri was something else altogether.

The only regret that clouded Robin's enjoyment of his walk was the way they had left without saying a word to Yuri. He could still clearly remember the evening of their hurried departure as if it was yesterday. The move had been suddenly decided the same evening they had learnt that they would get no more milk from Yuri after that day.

It had been partly prompted by Yahei and Tama coming to visit. Even so, they would never have been able to move that night had Amanejakki not turned up too. As the Little People stood beside the empty blue glass goblet gazing down on sleeping Yuri, they heard the sound of rustling leaves in the garden. Looking out through the lattice window, they saw Yahei and Amanejakki gesturing to them.

Amanejakki was spinning round and round the garden, gesticulating frantically. "Come on, hurry up! Come to my place! You can't stay there any more, surely..." he urged.

"But Yuri's sick. Are you saying we should leave her behind just like that?" responded Iris.

Whirling like crazy through the snow-bound garden, he gestured wildly, "But...when humans stop giving you milk, you have to leave immediately, don't you? That's the rule of your people."

Yahei and Tama joined in, "Quickly, hurry! Do as Amanejakki says and get ready to move right away. We'll carry you on our backs."

Balbo and Fern, Robin and Iris all looked at each other. It was true. There was no more milk and, as Amanejakki said, the time had come for them to leave.

"But... but what about Yuri? It's not as if it's all her fault."

But Fern, who had been staring hard at Amanejakki, turned to Balbo and said flatly, "Balbo, let's go. Ever since we began drinking out of the same cup as Yuri, I've been having a terrible premonition. We already started breaking the rule then. We can't stay here any longer. Iris and Robin, get ready to leave. We'll do as that little imp says and go with him. There's no other way."

Fern's voice was full of sorrow. They all went back to their home on the shelf, and she started putting on her new shoes. Balbo, Robin and Iris did as she said and started packing up their belongings.

The garden was already sunk in dusk when Amanejakki gestured, "Bring out your luggage."

It took all four of the Little People pushing as hard as they could to get the big blanket out of the window. Amanejakki instantly turned into a mini-whirlwind and whipped it clear. Yahei and Tama each took one of Balbo's and Fern's heavy trunks in their claws, and lifted them away. Amanejakki worked furiously transporting their bedding and kitchen equipment on numerous trips.

Finally, all that was left was Robin's book, but it was heavy and the Little People were too tired to carry it to the window.

"Let's leave it for Yuri. It can be our way of saying goodbye," Balbo said to Robin.

Robin began shaking his head, but then fell quiet for a few moments. At length he said, "No. I will leave it for Yuri, but as a sign that we'll be back one day."

Without a word, Iris selected the prettiest of the ribbons she herself had knitted, and put it in between its pages.

Coo coo! urged Yahei in a low voice.

The four Little People looked down on sick Yuri once more. Her eyes were closed.

"Yuri, when you're able to put milk here by the window for us every day again, we'll come back home, we promise!" said Balbo.

"Yuri, get better soon! We're leaving the blue glass goblet here for you," Fern added.

Robin and Iris were sobbing and said nothing.

How sad Yuri will be when she realizes we've gone! I wish there was some way we could tell her that we're not angry with her, Robin thought to himself.

Yuri, goodbye. I am not going to speak a single word until this terrible war is over and we're able to come back home to you. I am going to start knitting a prayer for you and the whole Moriyama family to survive these miserable times, promised Iris from the bottom of her heart.

But Yuri couldn't hear their faint farewells. As the Little People left the place that had been home for the past six months and climbed onto the pigeons' backs, they kept turning back for yet another last look.

Yahei took Balbo and Fern on his back, and Tama took Iris and Robin, both clad in their squirrel-skin coats. With a tremendous flapping of wings, they flew off over the larch forest.

Atop a small wooded hill the other side of the larch forest there stood a single small stone shrine. This was Amanejakki's home. It was very old and covered in rotting leaves, with thick moss growing over its foundations. He showed the Little People in through the back, while Yahei and Tama set off for home in the gathering darkness. (The living quarters were very cramped and it was impossible to invite their two big friends to stay over.)

Fern breathed a sigh of relief to find that this strange home was much cleaner and drier than she had expected. The family quickly began unpacking their belongings in the dim light of the handmade lamp.

Amanejakki went outside and brought them some clean, fresh water from a nearby stream. "Oh!" exclaimed Balbo upon seeing the bucket. It was a silver cup bearing the trademark of a famous British whisky manufacturer.

"But why?" Balbo began timidly.

The little imp gave him a cheeky wink, then took him into the cellar below the shrine. A few minutes later Balbo re-emerged, his face red with joy.

"Fern, Iris, Robin, come and have a look! We will be able to live here very well!"

The three took turns to peer into the cellar. In the dim light, they could see silver-foil cheese wrappers. There was enough cheese and honey down there for the Ashe family to live on for five years.

"How come, Amanejakki?" Fern asked.

"Where did you get all this food?" said Robin.

But the little imp just twisted his large mouth into a grin, and didn't answer. Balbo, Fern and little Robin were all bursting to know how on earth the cellar of this old shrine to a forgotten god deep in the mountains of Japan came to be full of cheese. Amanejakki in his fiery red waistcoat just laughed teasingly. Also in the cellar were several more of the squirrel-fur coats he had given to the Little People before.

Only Iris didn't ask any questions, and remained silent. Noticing that she had started knitting something in sparkling spider's silk, the Little People remembered Yuri. They spent their first night after the move drinking water and eating some of the fragrant cheese in silence.

Amanejakki gave the room he had been living in to Balbo and his family, and retreated into the larder where acorns, gingko nuts and nutmegs were stored.

Even though they were now living with Amanejakki, it was a long time before Balbo, Robin or even chatty Fern could get any information out of him as to how that cheese and the stylish bucket had come to be in the cellar. However, one day, without any prompting, he told Iris the story as she sat knitting in the shade of some violets behind the shrine.

Once upon a time, long, long ago, when Amanejakki had left his mother's house deep in the mountains and started living alone in these peaceful surroundings, he had built a cabin on the mountainside overlooking the lake. At the time there was not a single human living in the area and it was a land of rabbits and squirrels and foxes and pheasants and other creatures like Amanejakki himself.

Then early one summer, a lone human, tall with a white face, had come and built a cottage that looked quite like a mushroom. The human would come to his cottage every year for the summer months. He never killed any squirrels or rabbits or pheasants, but just napped quietly under the trees, or blew blue smoke through his nostrils, or sang songs, and over time Amanejakki grew steadily used to him. He really did seem to be fond of this place and everything in it, from the trees to the grass and even the spiders' webs.

One day, Amanejakki was overcome with curiosity about the source of the blue smoke that came out of the human's nose, and so while he was asleep under a tree, Amanejakki took the hot, brown stick that was in his mouth and, imitating him, put it to his own mouth, but the awful stink from it made him faint.

When he came to again, he was lying in bed beneath a round face that made a *tick tock* noise in the man's cottage. He made to jump up and run away, but his head spun and he couldn't get up. Luckily the big man was in the next room, and didn't come in to see him. Presently, the thing that was going *tick tock, tick tock* suddenly shouted out *dong dong* and the door beneath the round face sprang open and a small figure about the same height as himself came unhurriedly out. It was an elderly woman with grey hair and bent back. It was only much later that he learnt that she was one of the Little People and lived alone in the thing that was called a clock. The little old woman walked over to the window and climbed up to the windowsill where there was a blue glass goblet filled to the brim with something white.

A blue glass goblet? Iris started in surprise.

"Yes, a blue glass goblet, just like the one you had on your windowsill," said Amanejakki. "That big man only stayed in the mountains over the summer, but the grey-haired little woman lived in the clock in his cottage all year round. That's why, ever since I saw a similar type of clock arrive at the house you were living in, I was expecting one of your type to come out of it."

Iris opened her eyes wide in surprise.

Amanejakki puffed his chest out and said, "It was because of that little old woman that I knew that Little People like you could survive the winter without the milk in that blue glass by eating cheese made from it instead. And she also taught me how to tell the time and how to make warm coats from squirrel fur. And before she left, she gave me all the cheese and honey that's in the cellar here."

The hint of a smile appeared on Iris's face. She now knew for sure that she and her family were not the only Little People left in the world and, what's more, that this place deep in the mountains had been home to an old woman from England.

Amanejakki sensed that Iris had been gradually drawn into the story, and soon began to lose interest in it. "That Little Person went away. The big man took her back to their country. This all happened long ago. Since then other people have started living around here too, and the forests and thickets have been cleared to grow crops, and the rabbits and squirrels and foxes have all gone deeper into the mountains. Only I've stayed, since I have the cheese, and I thought that one day that little grey-haired old woman might come back."

He looked increasingly bored with the story, and now began spinning around the meadow of violets.

And the cottage? gestured Iris.

"The cottage... the cottage was reduced to ashes some time ago... a passing human stayed there and left something burning, so it caught fire and all that was left was ashes," he said, and disappeared off through meadow spinning like the wind.

Robin began wondering what Yuri was doing. Thinking of her lying sick in bed while he'd been having so much fun outside, he couldn't bear it any longer. He had already finished collecting the nectar from the flowers, so he took the path through the grass to check up on Aunt Toyo's house in the larch forest.

Just yesterday Yahei, who had recently moved with Tama to the woods near the little shrine, told him that Yuri had recovered from her illness and that he'd seen her going on her way to school these past two or three days. Unnoticed by anyone, Robin slipped into the garden of Aunt Toyo's house. Fresh green shoots were appearing on the tree where Yuri had made Tsutomu tie the ribbon for Yahei all those months ago, and he could see a woodpecker's tail feathers poking out of the round hole of its nest.

Robin looked up nostalgically at the lattice window. The blue glass was still there. And it was full of white milk. Robin couldn't believe his eyes! Yuri was putting milk out for them again! He rushed back to the little shrine and wasted no time in telling his mother, "Yuri's put some milk out for us by the window again! She hasn't forgotten us, she's putting milk out for us!"

Fern told him quietly, "I know that. Today is the third day she has put it there. I hope she keeps it up; if she manages it for seventy-seven days in a row, we'll be able to go back to her. But these are difficult times, so I'm not sure she'll be able to."

Neither Iris nor Balbo said anything. Even here in Amanejakki's little shrine beneath the trees, they had started hearing the faint sounds of war. Now and then a terrible siren would wail and send the humans running. There hadn't been any air raids around this peaceful lake yet, but the siren warning of enemy planes was reaching them. With the situation being like this, it would probably be even harder for Yuri to get hold of milk than it had been during the snowy winter.

"Robin, bring your pencil. Use it to make a mark on that pillar for every day that Yuri puts milk out for us, so that we'll know whether or not she manages to keep it up for seventy-seven days," Fern told him.

Robin did as he was told and made three marks on the shrine's old wooden pillar. And he promised Fern and the others that from now on he would drop by Aunt Toyo's house after his daily walk to check whether the milk had been left by the window there.

COME HOME, LITTLE PEOPLE!

Robin made his marks on the shrine's pillar in blocks of five, like so: ̶H̶H̶. Soon there were seven blocks, then eight. He borrowed Amanejakki's bucket so he could take the milk from the blue glass goblet back to his family.

It was the same powdered milk that Yuri had given them before. She had asked her mother to send her a tin of powdered milk for Balbo and his family, and made it up for them in their glass every day. After a while, the contents of the glass began disappearing, which made her heart sing.

"Come home, Little People! If you're still alive, please come home to me!"

Seeing the way the familiar blue glass sparkled with new

life, Yuri sensed that her plea had reached the hearts of the four Little People. *However hungry I get, this time I'll put some milk out by the window for you every day without fail for as long as I possibly can!*

As they drank the milk Yuri had started leaving out for them again after so long, the Little People thought how delicious it was. Robin made up his mind to take the silver bucket to collect the milk every day.

One day in June, when there were ten blocks of marks on the pillar, Robin found the glass on the windowsill empty. It was a nasty wet afternoon, but he had set out cheerfully with a large magnolia leaf covering his head, only to return to the shrine dispirited with the empty bucket.

"It looks like Yuri's run out of milk again," he said sadly.

"What a pity! If she'd managed to keep it up for another twenty-seven days, we'd have been able to go home to her. But in these terrible times, it can't be helped," Fern said, disappointed. However nice this shrine was to live in, it grew damp and chilly inside whenever it rained for any length of time. Noticing Balbo holding his knees in silence, she sighed and said, "Balbo, wrap your legs in the blanket so your knees don't catch cold."

Balbo was stitching a pair of simple shoes for Amanejakki using the skin from some smoked salmon in the cellar for leather.

At his side, his daughter Iris was knitting in silence. Ever since they had left Yuri she had kept her promise not to utter a single word, and to spend all her time knitting one long rainbow-coloured ribbon, until the war ended and they could go home to her. Iris had often heard from her mother that

162

the knitting needles she had inherited from her grandmother Beatrice Belladonna Took had magical powers, although Fern couldn't say what form that magical power might take.

Iris's rainbow ribbon grew longer and longer and coiled onto the floor like a river. One day, as she worked her needles furiously, it occurred to her that if she carried on knitting eventually the ribbon would grow long enough to girth the entire world they lived in. When that happened, all the terrible wars on earth would end and the suffering of all the many children like Yuri would be no more. In order for Yuri to be happy, peace had to reign in the entire Moriyama family, and for everyone in Japan to be happy peace had to reign throughout the entire world.

That's right, Iris, keep knitting. Don't talk, just keep knitting! When this ribbon grows long enough to encircle the entire earth, war will end and people will be happy again... whispered the mysterious ivory knitting needles as they moved in Iris's hands like live creatures. *But why? Why me? How come I, little me, can do something so big?* Iris wondered without allowing her hands to rest even for a moment.

Amanejakki, normally so naughty, now became Iris's devoted assistant. He wanted so much to help her that he could hardly contain himself. As quick-witted as ever, he now went all over the mountain gathering piles of the fine thread she wanted, just as once he had brought her bird feathers. He gathered cocoons from the oak silk moths and spun them into thread for her. As he span frantically, the strong and pretty thread grew quickly and he persuaded Fern to give him some of the dye to make it rainbow-coloured.

Thank you, Amanejakki! Iris would gesture each time he brought it to her. Sometimes she would grace him, and only

163

him, with a smile, which caused him to blush and rush off around the mountain like the wind.

The pencil marks on the pillar in the little shrine continued increasing in number, as the Little People felt Yuri's insistent call to them, *Come home! Come home!*

One day, just as Robin was on his way out with the silver bucket to collect the milk, Balbo said to him, "Robin, why don't you write Yuri a letter? Maybe it's about time we let her know that we are safe and well."

And so Robin took his time over writing her a letter. He used two pages from the notebook before he was finished.

"*Coo coo!* I'll take it for you," said Yahei, who'd been waiting outside.

"*Coo coo!* Let me take it!" added Tama.

But Amanejakki grabbed the letter and, spinning round and round into a little whirlwind, went straight over to Yuri's house. But she was far away at the time, cutting grass on a mountainside with her classmates from school.

Yuri wielded her scythe lightly, rapidly felling the grass. Under the glare of the July sun, the fragrance of the freshly cut grass grew stronger. She was no longer wearing her "Korean shoes" but the same straw sandals as her classmates, treading down the grass with her suntanned feet. None of the other children helped her, but now she was able to cut grass and bundle it up all by herself. The school provided the children with potatoes and sweet potatoes as snacks, and whoever cut the most grass would be given the biggest, so they all brushed away their sweat and competed with each other to cut the most.

"Ouch!!!"

Suddenly Tsutomu let out a yell, and pressed his hand towel over his leg. His shin had been cut by a tiny spinning whirlwind. The others shot him sympathetic looks, but didn't stop their work. Then the pile of grass he'd cut flew up into the air and over to where the other children were at work. Tsutomu lost his temper.

"Hey that's not fair! Stop nicking my grass!"

Yuri looked at Tsutomu in surprise as he angrily grabbed some grass from her pile and stormed back over to his own.

"Tsutomu, don't—" she started, but then all of a sudden her eyes lit up. There on the ground by her feet where the grass had blown over a moment ago were two small white sheets of paper. *Robin!* Her heart leapt as she picked up the familiar sheets of notebook paper.

She no longer cared how much of her grass Tsutomu took. All she could think of was the letter from the Little People, and she glanced restlessly around wondering whether Robin and Iris were nearby. But there was no sign of any of them in amongst the pampas grass and gentian blooms.

Carrying the grass on their backs, the children went back to the school, where one by one their loads were weighed. Chewing on the small sweet potato she was given, Yuri climbed up to the mountain pass as fast as she could to read Robin's letter.

Yuri, we are fine. We was happy to get your milk. Pleez keep giving us milk for seventy-seven days. We made frends with Amanejakki. We're with you Yuri. Balbo, Fern and Iris want to come home quik. See you soon.

R.

It was quite a long letter for Robin. And for the first time she felt she could tell her mother about the Little People having left her. While she was ill, and even since she had recovered, she couldn't bring herself to write the truth in her letters home. How could she tell her mother, who had entrusted the Little People's care to her all those years ago in the little book room, that she had lost them? She couldn't add to her mother's troubles, not after she'd stayed in Tokyo despite the terrible air raids in order to keep sending supplies to her father "inside", and after her eldest son Tetsu had joined the army.

Yuri carefully folded up Robin's letter and put it in her air raid bag along with all the letters from home, and the miniature picture book that Robin had left behind. Tucked inside the book, along with the pretty ribbon from Iris, was a photo of Tetsu that Toko had sent her recently. It was the photo that Yuri had taken of him on Benten Island, and had come out very well.

I'll definitely get the Little People back. Of course I'll keep putting out milk for them for seventy-seven days in a row!

This time Yuri was determined to make the can of powdered milk she'd received from Katsuko in Hondo last for seventy-seven days. If the powdered milk alone could last for about fifty days, she would somehow manage to get hold of goat's milk for the remaining twenty or so days...

By mid-August, there were nine blocks of Robin's pencil marks on the pillar, and Yuri could see the bottom of the can of milk. It was the Bon festival and school was out, and all she could think of was how to get hold of some goat's milk.

One day just after lunch Tsutomu's mother came to Aunt Toyo's house. She had come in a hurry, not even putting on her sedge hat, and was telling Aunt Toyo something, her voice shrill. Suddenly the two women burst into tears. Scared out of her wits, Yuri went looking for Granny Oto and found her quietly weeping out front.

"Yuri, Yuri—come here!"

Hearing Aunt Toyo calling her, she went fearfully through. Aunt Toyo never cried, but now her big eyes were filled with tears.

"Yuri," she said, as if wringing the words out of herself, "Japan has lost the war. There was a broadcast by His Imperial Majesty, and Mrs Toyama heard it..."

"Yuri, poor you! It's been so hard on you, and now we've gone and lost... and all those people died for nothing," wailed Tsutomu's mother, overcome with emotion.

Yuri too began to cry, but deep down a feeling of joy began bubbling up inside her. She'd never believed she'd live to see the end of the war, but it was now over. *I'll be able to see Daddy again... and Mummy and Tetsu and Shin... and I'll go back to Tokyo and we'll all live together again!*

That night Yuri saw lights coming on all over the mountain, sparkling in the dark. The closest one must have been from Tsutomu's house. Aunt Toyo must have noticed too, for she took down the heavy blackout curtain from the kitchen window. As if drawn by the lights, the two of them went up to the mountain pass and gazed down on their pretty reflections in the lake.

"I really wish Granny Oto could see this!" Yuri said from the bottom of her heart.

Aunt Toyo looked at her. Then they smiled at each other, and went back to their brightly lit house.

Now if only Robin and the others would come home! That's all I ask for! Yuri thought feelingly as she got into bed.

DARK DAYS

The war might have ended, but for Yuri life went on as before without any big changes.

A letter from her mother in Tokyo arrived giving the happy news that her father had been acquitted of the crime of treason, and had at long last been allowed to leave prison. Worryingly, though, it also said that he was ill and would have to stay in hospital for a while. Most disappointing of all, nowhere in that letter did it say, "I'm coming to get you, Yuri." When the war had ended on 15th August, Yuri had thought she would soon be able to go back home to Tokyo, but...

Now that the hope of going home had been kindled in her, Yuri couldn't bear to stay here in Nojiri a moment longer, and she felt increasingly irritable as the days went by. But there was one bright point: she'd been able to make up with her friend and classmate Tsutomu.

Around 20th August, she'd realized there was just one spoonful of milk left in the bottom of the can, and she was suddenly seized with anxiety. Robin had written that she should continue for seventy-seven days, but there were still twenty-five or -six days to go. What if she couldn't leave any milk for them? There was nothing for it—she would have to swallow her pride and go to Tsutomu's house.

She went clutching Aunt Toyo's sickle firmly in her hand. *Somehow I've got to persuade Tsutomu to let me cut grass in exchange for some milk!* She rehearsed over and over again what she would say to him, and also imagined herself flinching at being coldly rejected by his family. But she couldn't give up, she just *had* to get hold of some goat's milk somehow or other.

As she climbed up the mountain path, she bumped into Tsutomu coming the other way with a bundle of grass on his back. Unthinkingly, she came to an abrupt halt. Tsutomu looked at her in surprise. He looked tired and somewhat dejected.

Yuri didn't say anything and just stood there glaring at him.

"Yuri," he said after a few moments. "I'm sorry... I didn't mean..." he mumbled nervously, his eyes downcast.

Yuri was so taken aback that the words she'd been rehearsing over and over again came tumbling easily out. "Tsutomu, let me cut grass for you! And in exchange give me some milk."

Tsutomu stared at her, flabbergasted. "You *still* want some goat's milk?"

"Yes, I do. I only need a little. But I want some every day."

She was so determined that in the end Tsutomu had to give in and agreed to let her have about half a bowlful every day. They went together to the mountainside to cut grass daily until school started again in September, and in return she received some milk for the Little People.

"You're lucky Yuri. Your dad and your brothers are alive," Tsutomu said to her one day. Another of his elder brothers had recently been taken by the army too. "I don't know what's good and what isn't any more. It's true that I happily cheered *Banzai!* when he went off to the front—but then, when I think that he won't be coming back either, I get so angry I can't stand it any more. My Mum doesn't say anything, but sometimes she just sits in a daze, a far-off look in her eyes. I can't bear seeing her like that while she's out at work in the vegetable fields."

"My brother Tetsu hasn't come back yet," Yuri told him. "What he said was true, you know. There's nothing good about war at all. As soon as he gets back, he'll come and get me."

Then the two of them promised that, come September, they would start collecting firewood in the mountains for Tsutomu's house and Aunt Toyo's house.

By now there were thirteen blocks of marks on the pillar in the shrine.

Fern breathed a sigh of relief as Robin again returned with milk Yuri had left by the window for them. "Oh, good! If she keeps it up for another twelve days, we'll be able to go back to her."

Robin pouted. "But I don't want to go back. I want to stay living here with Amanejakki." He was now utterly captivated by the dizzying speed with which his friend could see through to what was in people's hearts.

"Don't say such stupid things!" Fern grew really angry at her son's response. "Do you think you can stay here for ever? Think about your father's health!" It was only the beginning of September, but Balbo's legs hurt so much that he now spent all day in bed. During their stay in the mountains the children had grown strong and suntanned, but Balbo and Fern had become visibly weaker. "Yahei told me that Japan ended up losing the war. Everyone who moved from the city to the countryside will soon be going back. If Yuri suddenly goes back to Tokyo, what on earth shall we do?"

Robin grinned. "In that case, we can stay here with Amanejakki until his cellar is empty, then go back to Tokyo with Yahei."

Fern lost her temper. "How can you say that, Robin? Think about it. Right now, even if Yuri was looking straight at us, she wouldn't be able to see us. Until she's completed her atonement by putting out milk for us seventy-seven days in a row, we're invisible to her. If she goes away now, we will never see her again. I don't want that to happen!"

Robin stared at his mother. Then he gave a mocking laugh and went outside.

Mid-September came around. The seventy-seventh day had finally arrived, and Yuri's hand shook as she poured the goat's milk into the freshly washed blue glass goblet.

Every day when she came back from the mountains she would check the glass by the window, but she had not even once seen any of the Little People there. Nevertheless, every day the blue glass sparkled prettily, and the milk Yuri poured into it would disappear from one moment to the next. This was the only evidence she had that the Little People had been taking it.

Yuri bundled up the kindling that she and Tsutomu had brought from the mountain and carried it to the shed, which by now was almost full. Afterwards she went to her room and looked at the window in surprise. The blue glass goblet she had placed there earlier was nowhere to be seen. *What if it's fallen down and broken?* she thought in alarm, and looked below the window. But it wasn't there either.

She heard a rustling of dry leaves in the back garden and ran outside in her bare feet, just in time to catch sight of something blue sparkling just by the start of the larch forest. As she approached, a little whirlwind spinning round and round, with none other than the blue glass goblet sparkling at its centre, moved off into the trees.

"Wait! Give me back my glass! Wait!"

Forgetting how much her bare feet hurt, Yuri ran after it as fast as she could. Beyond the dense woodland, the big evening sun was beginning to set as she ran into the cold golden light of the forest. There was a flapping of wings as a couple of pigeons, one grey and one white, flew up into the air.

Then she noticed a small crumbling stone shrine. There were voices like the rustling of leaves coming from inside it. Suddenly something about the size of a large grasshopper surged towards her feet. It was little Fern. Startled, Yuri crouched down and scooped her up in her hands. Fern's hair was dishevelled and she was gasping for breath.

What happened next was something that Yuri would never forget as long as she lived. The small blue whirlwind started spinning around her, round and round and round until she became quite dizzy, and then out of the crumbling little shrine flew Balbo, still wrapped in his quilt, followed by Iris, still knitting something sparkly. And last of all came Robin, a silver bucket on his head.

"Amanejakki, go faster! Faster!" shouted Fern in a thin, shrill voice from Yuri's palm. In a flash the whirlwind stopped and the blue glass goblet wobbled on the path like a spinning top coming to a halt.

Dazed, Yuri noticed that it was empty. After a few moments Fern shouted at her, "Yuri, please take us home now!"

Yuri came to herself with a start, picked up the old worn blanket where it had fallen on the ground and gently spread it out so that Fern and the others could get on it. A cricket chirred in the grass.

Holding the Little People on the blanket in one hand and the blue glass in the other, Yuri went home in the deepening sunset.

There was a rustling in the grass, but Yuri didn't see anything. In her joy at the Little People coming home with her after such a long absence, she didn't notice the strange little figure crying there in the undergrowth.

Hidden in the grass, Amanejakki buried his face in his arm and wept.

If he had done nothing, Robin and Iris would no doubt have stayed living with him for evermore. Today, the seventy-seventh day, Robin had refused to go to collect the milk from Yuri.

"I'm not going back to Yuri's. I'm staying here with you!" Robin told him.

Amanejakki had looked away. If Robin had told him "Goodbye!" he would have gone and spilt Yuri's milk so that he wouldn't have been able to leave.

Then he looked over at Iris, sitting there silently knitting the sparkling ribbon as she always did. Her eyes said *Me too! I'll stay here. I'll keep knitting without uttering a single word until this ribbon is long enough to encircle the world. And I'll stay here with you while I knit!*

If Iris's eyes had been saying *Goodbye!*, Amanejakki would never have let her go back to Yuri. If he hadn't loved these Little People so much, he would have stopped them from leaving. But as it was, he had gone straight out and snatched up the blue glass goblet full of milk that Yuri had left by the window, and brought it to Fern in the shrine.

Fern had exclaimed, "Yuri! Oh! I'll be able to see Yuri again!" and dashed outside. Amanejakki had splattered the milk around and driven Balbo and Iris and little Robin out after her.

And the Little People had gone away, leaving him alone once more.

The two pigeons, up on a high branch, began singing their evening song as, unknown to anyone, poor Amanejakki sat beneath the grass, black in the darkness, and wept.

Once again the first snowfall of winter came to Nojiri.

Every day, Yuri waited for a letter from her mother telling her she could come home. But in Toko's letters to her she never once wrote the words "Come home". Neither did she write anything about Tetsu. All she told Yuri was that her father was still in hospital and that her other brother Shin was fine, nothing more. In her letters to Aunt Toyo, though, she wrote in great detail that Yuri's father had tuberculosis due to his prolonged period of confinement and terrible malnutrition, and that his prognosis was not good.

One day when the snow was falling thick and fast, someone came to visit Yuri. It was Katsuko from Hondo. She had often visited Yuri when she had been sick, and Aunt Toyo gave her a warm welcome as she turned up covered in snow, leading the goat behind her.

"I came to say goodbye," she said, coming straight to the point. "My friends have all gone back to Tokyo already. I thought I could maybe ask you to keep this goat. To tell the truth, I should have left it at the house where I've been staying, but I really wanted Yuri to have it."

Aunt Toyo accepted the snow-covered goat and took it away into the earthen-floored part of the house.

"Have you heard about Tetsu?"

Yuri shook her head.

"You poor thing. Your brother was killed in action on 8th August. If only the war had ended just a week earlier, he would have come home safe and sound." Katsuko didn't cry. She spoke quietly and dispassionately, looking straight at Yuri. "I'm sorry to be telling this to one so young, but I just have to inform someone who knows him. Tetsu won't be coming home. Ever. A friend of his told me: 'On 8th August, Tetsu Moriyama sacrificed his nineteen years of life for our country', is what he said."

Aunt Toyo came back in and, putting her arm around Katsuko's rigid shoulders, sat her down by the sunken hearth. Then she wiped the tears from Yuri's cheeks with the rough palms of her hands.

"Is that so? I'm so sorry for Toko, too." Big tears dripped from Aunt Toyo's eyes into the ashes of the fire.

Little Yuri noticed that Granny Oto, too, was weeping silently as she lay in bed. And their world was enveloped in the faint rustle of the falling snow. Finally Katsuko stood up. Aunt Toyo tried to hold her back, telling her to stay, but Katsuko started getting herself ready to leave.

Yuri ran into the other room and came back with her air raid bag and a paper package.

"This was from Tetsu to you," she said, pressing the package into Katsuko's hands. "He brought me some sparklers, and told me to give half of them to you, and so I'm giving them to you now." Then she took a small book out of her air raid bag. Tucked inside the pages was a photograph, which she handed to Katsuko.

A pained look briefly crossed Katsuko's face. She packed away the paper package and photograph, and put her hand on the door.

"I'm taking some of the rice I grew here back to Tokyo with me. I'll give some of it to your mother and father."

Katsuko went off alone in the thick snow. Just like the day she had seen Tetsu off, Yuri watched Katsuko with her pack on her back quickly disappear from sight along the mountain path during the first heavy snowfall of the year.

YURI GOES HOME

———

T he long, long winter came to an end, and once again spring came to Lake Nojiri. On the path beside the school, where the cherries, peaches and plums were briefly in bloom, Yuri was waiting for her mother Toko.

She had been in year three when she came here, and had already entered year five this April. Her father, Tatsuo, was finally over the worst of his illness and Toko was at last able to leave him to come and collect her daughter. Having finished talking to Yuri's teachers about her school transfer, she came out of the office and said, "Yuri, your teacher told me that when you first arrived here you were quite a weakling and a burden on the rest of your classmates when doing the grass-cutting work. However, you soon grew as strong as all the others, and now the classroom is going to feel really lonely without you. Tsutomu especially is going to miss you, she said."

Yuri was thin but had grown tall, and Toko thought she now looked as though she could depend on her.

"But the one who's going to miss me most when I leave is the goat Jiro. The goat that Katsuko left with us—" said Yuri, then clamped her mouth shut.

Together, they climbed the path where dandelions were in flower up to Aunt Toyo's house.

"It was good of Katsuko to remember that glass goblet," Toko said. "She came to see us out of the blue, together with a young foreign woman. Yuri, don't you think it's amazing? That foreign woman was the daughter of Miss MacLachlan's niece. That means that the Miss MacLachlan who left Balbo and the others with your father when he was a little boy was her great-aunt. And that same Miss MacLachlan is still alive and well, now aged eighty-four, living in England. She showed me a colour photograph of her standing in a field of pale-purple heather, eagerly awaiting the day Balbo and his family come home."

Yuri caught her breath. "Do we have to give the Little People back?" This was something that had never occurred to her, even in her dreams.

"Well, it's up to us... but you know, that young Miss MacLachlan who came to see us had been leaving milk in a blue glass goblet exactly like the one we have in the window of the hotel she was staying in. Katsuko happened to be visiting a friend in the same hotel and saw it. Since it was rather unusual she asked her friend about it, and was doubly surprised when it turned out that the woman was looking for someone by the name of Moriyama."

"But... but I don't want to give them back! I lost them once and they only just came back to me!"

"I heard about that," said Toko quietly. "Katsuko told me they'd left you while you were ill, and we all cried over that... me, Katsuko and also the young Miss MacLachlan... and making you give them back now, after all this time looking after them..." She went on hesitantly, "But Yuri, back in Tokyo the little book room doesn't exist any more, you know. How can you give them a safe place where they can live peacefully now and in the future?"

Yuri couldn't answer. Toko continued disconsolately, "Tetsu still treasured the Little People even after growing up, didn't he? Katsuko was really sad about that, you know. She wished she'd been able to hear about them from Tetsu himself."

The two of them walked in silence through the larch forest, fragrant with fresh buds.

"But then why did Miss MacLachlan leave them behind in the first place?" asked Yuri accusingly.

Toko averted her eyes. With a distant look, she answered, "You know, Miss MacLachlan decided to come to Japan because she had heard it was a small, peaceful country where the 'pure heart' that Westerners had forgotten still existed. That was in about the twentieth year of Meiji, around 1888. She left her native England to come all the way to our country with the intention of dedicating her life to being an educator here. But instead of this 'pure heart', what she found in Japan was an intense, almost insane drive to catch up with Western civilization. During her twenty years here, the Japan she had sought gradually disappeared. She couldn't bear the fact that the poor, who were pure of heart, were oppressed by the military, government officials

180

and the rich. She wrote about this for a magazine, and as a result she was forced to leave the country. At that time, Fern was already expecting a child, and taking her and Balbo with her in third class on the ship was out of the question, and so she gave them to Tatsuo, who was the pupil she most trusted to look after them. This is what the young Miss MacLachlan told Katsuko and me not long ago. And she also told us that her great-aunt, the elder Miss MacLachlan, never doubted for a moment that, even during that terrible war, Tatsuo or whoever he had entrusted the Little People to had kept them alive and well somewhere in Japan. So, Yuri, let's send Balbo and his family back to England. Daddy's come home safely, so now let's make one elderly Western woman's dream come true. We should let her know that in the Japan she trusted, the pure heart needed to keep the Little People alive did exist."

Yuri quickened her pace. Perhaps she should send the Little People back to the old lady in England. Adults would think that was a beautiful thing to do. But Yuri didn't think so. Why should she have to give them and the blue glass goblet up, just when she'd got them back?

She stormed up the hill so fast that Toko couldn't keep up and was left behind on the mountain path, alone with the strains of a bush warbler's song.

The day came for Yuri to go home. Aunt Toyo and blind Granny Oto both looked as if they had suddenly aged, and they looked very sad, too.

Yuri took her mother through the larch forest to Tsutomu's house to say goodbye, and Toko and Tsutomu's mother had a long talk, while neither Tsutomu nor Yuri said anything. Then it was time for Yuri and her mother to leave, and Tsutomu promised that this autumn too he would cut enough grass to feed Jiro the goat over the winter.

When they got back to Aunt Toyo's house, Yuri took out the old basket and started packing for the Little People. The night before, she had told Balbo and Fern and Robin and Iris that she would be taking them back to Tokyo with her, and also about Miss MacLachlan. To begin with the Little People hadn't understood what she was talking about. Even now Yuri wasn't happy about sending the Little People back to England, and she hadn't been able to explain the situation very well to them.

"So we'll be able to see Miss MacLachlan again?" When Fern and Balbo finally understood what Yuri was getting at, a strange expression of sadness mixed with joy spread over their faces.

"That's right. And all I'll be left with is the blue glass goblet."

Iris continued knitting without a word. And a hint of a smile flitted across Robin's face.

Yuri spread the blue jumper that her mother had knitted for her over the bottom of the basket. It had been new when she came here, although it was now quite grimy from mountain life. But the wool was still soft and pliable, and it was the best possible cushion for the Little People.

She wrapped the blue glass in a clean handkerchief and put it in her own luggage. This would be her only memento of the Little People. Then she stood on the long chest and peered on top of the shelf. Only Balbo and Fern were waiting there, their travel preparations complete. Yuri gently transferred the two of them to the basket.

"What about Robin and Iris?" she asked.

Balbo shook his head sadly. Fern hid her face in her hands and crouched down on the floor of the basket. Robin and Iris had run away! Suddenly realizing this, Yuri rushed to the thicket. The crumbling small shrine sat hushed as before.

"Robin! Iris! Come back! Come back to Tokyo with me!"

"Robin! Iris! Come back!"

Yuri's voice dissipated in the forest in vain, and there was no answer.

Two pigeons rose from the treetops with a flapping of wings.

"Robin! Iris! Come back!"

Yuri put her mouth close up to the entrance to the shrine and called for all she was worth. But there was no reply, just the call of the grasses rustling in the evening breeze. Yuri went back to the house.

And she and Toko went to the station, taking just Balbo and Fern with them.

As the whistle on Yuri's train blew as it pulled out of Kashiwabara Station, the little imp Amanejakki was dancing around the little shrine in the forest drunk with joy at finding Robin and Iris sitting there waiting for him.

"You came back! I bet you're sad at leaving Yuri. But still, you want to live here with me, right?"

He danced round and round and round the woods with his eyes glittering and hair flying, a fiery red little whirlwind.

PUSHKIN CHILDREN'S BOOKS

Just as we all are, children are fascinated by stories. From the earliest age, we love to hear about monsters and heroes, romance and death, disaster and rescue, from every place and time.

We created Pushkin Children's Books to share these tales from different languages and cultures with younger readers, and to open the door to the wide, colourful worlds these stories offer.

From picture books and adventure stories to fairy tales and classics, and from fifty-year-old bestsellers to current huge successes abroad, the books on the Pushkin Children's list reflect the very best stories from around the world, for our most discerning readers of all: children.

THE WITCH IN THE BROOM CUPBOARD
AND OTHER TALES
PIERRE GRIPARI

Illustrated by Fernando Puig Rosado

'Wonderful... funny, tender and daft'
David Almond

━━━━━━

THE STORY OF THE BLUE PLANET
ANDRI SNÆR MAGNASON

Illustrated by Áslaug Jónsdóttir

'A Seussian mix of wonder, wit and gravitas'
The New York Times

━━━━━━

SHOLA AND THE LIONS
BERNARDO ATXAGA

Illustrated by Mikel Valverde

'Gently ironic stories... totally charming'
Independent

━━━━━━

THE POINTLESS LEOPARD:
WHAT GOOD ARE KIDS ANYWAY?
COLAS GUTMAN

Illustrated by Delphine Perret

'Lively, idiomatic and always entertaining...
a decidedly offbeat little book'
Robert Dunbar, *Irish Times*

POCKETY: THE TORTOISE WHO LIVED AS SHE PLEASED

FLORENCE SEYVOS

Illustrated by Claude Ponti

'A treasure – a real find – and one of the most enjoyable
children's books I've read in a while… This is a tortoise
that deserves to win every literary race'
Observer

THE LETTER FOR THE KING

TONKE DRAGT

'Gripping from its opening moment onwards, this
award-winning book doesn't miss a beat from its
thrilling beginning to its satisfying ending'
Julia Eccleshare

THE PILOT AND THE LITTLE PRINCE

PETER SÍS

'With its extraordinary, sophisticated illustrations,
its poetry and the historical detail of the text, this
book will reward readers of any age over eight'
Sunday Times

SAVE THE STORY

GULLIVER · ANTIGONE · CAPTAIN NEMO · DON JUAN
GILGAMESH · THE BETROTHED · THE NOSE
CYRANO DE BERGERAC · KING LEAR · CRIME AND PUNISHMENT

'An amazing new series from Pushkin Press in which
literary, adult authors retell classics (with terrific
illustrations) for a younger generation'
Daily Telegraph

THE CAT WHO CAME IN OFF THE ROOF

ANNIE M.G. SCHMIDT

'Guaranteed to make anyone 7-plus to 107 who likes to
curl up with a book and a cat purr with pleasure'
The Times

THE OKSA POLLOCK SERIES

ANNE PLICHOTA AND CENDRINE WOLF

Part 1 · *The Last Hope*

Part 2 · *The Forest of Lost Souls*

Part 3 · *The Heart of Two Worlds*

'A feisty heroine, lots of sparky tricks and evil opponents
could fill a gap left by the end of the Harry Potter series'
Daily Mail

THE VITELLO SERIES

KIM FUPZ AAKESON

Illustrated by Niels Bo Bojesen

'Full of quirky humour and an anarchic sense
of fun that children will love'
Booktrust

A HOUSE WITHOUT MIRRORS

MÅRTEN SANDÉN

Illustrated by Moa Schulman

'A classic story that has it all'
Dagens Nyheter